VICTORIA J HUNT

Author & Illustrator

Sally In The Woods

A ghost story and legend retold

Ghostly apparitions have been reported on the road through Brown Folly woods and should you ever visit you will feel a prescence, many stories and beliefs have been told, from the wood choppers strange account of his memeory in the valley, this fantasy story unfolds and tells a tale of a ghost story that has a deeper and desperate need to complette a mission that failed centuries ago.

THE AUTHOR

Since a child I have written and drawn, my first book took me years to be brave enough to publish and I still feel nervous to share my work, I write for pleasure and love to research and bring places I have explored into my books, I am inspired by historical places and facts and my love of nature and art. I studied literature and art and worked in the world of fashion before I had my own family. I now work with autistic children as a support worker and write books. I hope you, the reader enjoy my books.

Other Books

The Revenge Of Merga Bein

The Little Yew Tree Witch

The Curate The Witch & The Casket, Amie's Ghost

Tetonti & The Grand Quest

Dolly Mouse & Friends

An orphan from the woods taken by a coven steels the Lebkuchen and a name from a grave, she takes the boys heart with the blond curls and a chain of events begins, nothing can stop the revenge of Merga Bein and her love for Alderbert, entwined with the past Merga regrets her dealings with the demon Lilith, can she survive her curse and destroy the demons path. A romantic historical and magical tale, with a touch of horror and an abundance of charming characters, a world of warlocks and witches, with love, friendship and hope, from the Levante to the millers boy a fabulous journey with a dark and sinister twist and castles in the sky.

SALLY IN THE WOODS

Princess Meriiti 700 BC

Princess Meriiti was born on a sacred day she was considered a Princess of the Gods and her people believed she was sent for a reason, from a small child she was different and learnt all about the world, she experimented with ideas and saw things differently than most, the Princess was obsessed with the planets and stars and she seemed able to predict the winds and moons. She was loved by her people and lived a rich life by the huge River Nile, their settlement was large and her father the King ruled his people fairly yet sternly, her mother the Queen was beautiful and kind and her many siblings each felt special with their varied roles, the Princess explored her lands more as she grew older and on her eighth birthday she visited a sacred mountain, upon the mountain she heard the Gods story of a magical place on earth. Meriiti was more than intrigued and knew it was her purpose to go to the enchanting place with a waterfall of time. Meriiti lingered on the mountain that day and she met a boy who was shy and bear like in his ways, she chatted to him all about this wonderful place that the Gods had described and said when the time came, she would travel the seas, deserts, mountains and plains in search of the woodlands and find the place the Gods wished her to visit, Meriiti reluctantly left the bear like boy on the mountain waving and smiling, she thought him lovely but had to go, often she would think of him and hoped to see him again, the years rolled on though and she could not find him again. Princess Meriiti's people were from the land before the great Pharaohs, a small and gentle tribe they longed for the world they had been promised in the prophecy, they held the book of Moirai that they carried with great care, they were the protectors and named the Star Gazers and they waited for a sign. One night the stars and skies gave a dazzling display of colours, the people took this as their sign and Princess Meriiti the chosen one was sent with a large swathe of her people, they would search for the waterfalls of time, it was there they were foretold to leave the book of Moirai and travel back to the time of the Gods. The intriguing Neolithic folk began their journey knowing they would never return, they searched on always in hope for many centuries with the Princess Meriiti as their guide and council. They would lose many and gain a few on their travels and with each changing wind and year they grew closer to the northern hemispheres, where they sought their promised land.

THE BOY ONCE CALLED TOMOSA
700 BC

Long ago there lived a young boy called Tomosa he wandered the hills of his land for years alone in search of his lost family he had never known. One day he wandered deep in thought when he by chance bumped into a young maiden on a mountain, she told him she spoke with the Gods about a place far way and one day she would travel there, Tomosa thought her the most beautiful creature he had ever seen, afraid and unsure of his feelings and with only a few words he said nothing and the maiden was gone, Tomosa would visit the mountain many times in hope she would be there upon as she was that day. Tomosa was cared for by a bear family deep in the forest, so he struggled with human speech and manners, Tomosa started to watch for hours from a far on how his kind behaved and communicated, he became more and more intrigued and his passion for language and knowledge grew. Tomosa would eventually become a scholar of words and would write many wonderful scripts both in fables and poems. In his heart though he always thought of the woodlands and mountains as his home and would often return to the remote countryside and always he searched for her, one year in desperation he fled in search of the place she described in detail with such passion. Tomosa would meet many people and creatures on his journey and with each story of pity he would help and with each injury or peril he would save them, he became known through the lands as a saviour and saint, the Gods chose Tomosa as the one with the kindest and bravest heart, they gave him immortality, a soul so precious could not leave their world. Tomosa would continue to search and search for the one person he loved, he remembered her beautiful soft brown eyes and flowing hair, her sweet delicate ways and her pretty name Meriiti. Many moons and centuries later he found the woods and the place described by Meriiti, yet she again had gone, so Tomosa exhausted waited, he built a Folly from the deepest brown wood and spent his time carving the stories he had seen and he carved his Meriiti and there he would stay, his spirit lingered until the day he would again walk the earth as a boy and finally find his sweet Meriiti.

THE BOOK OF MOIRAI

In a forgotten time the world was in turmoil the Gods in dispute over the smallest and largest of things, torn between human and beast, centaurs, unicorns, manticores, mermaids and more all battled for their place, each ravaged by war torn worlds they faced extinction, man would take over and the beast would be cast aside as nothing more than a slave or dish to be served. A small group of Gods unknown to many would try to keep the mythical and magical human half beasts in existence and found places deeply hidden in the forests, mountains and oceans to keep their secret, a sacred few would span the world, enough to remember the laws of nature and balance and help save the fragile earth from the senseless, erratic and thoughtless actions of humans. Each of the creatures were placed by a sacred spring and waterfall that formed a porthole to different times and places. Knowing the creatures would struggle to keep their place on Earth, the creatures adapted to forms to fit into their ever changing worlds, in this way they were of little suspicion, the Fauns and Centaurs though would always remain the same half human half beast they would roam between times on the Earth to survive. These mythical amazing creatures would gallop through the ancient woods and would use the magical Dell for centuries, each one immortal, they carried the secrets and the knowledge of the woods. Hartol was a descendant from an ancient herd of Unicorns, he was a white stag as pure as snow and would live for thousands of years, clever and bright he inspired the woodland creatures. Hartol the protector of the Dell and woodlands could feel himself changing as the threat of the destruction grew, he felt more powerful and began to look for ways to stop the world from moving on. One day a strange yet godly human would pass through his woodland domain, Hartol was curious of his strange presence, they would talk for many days and nights, entranced by the godly mans knowledge and care, Hartol showed him the book of Moirai a book made by the Gods, with the words that could change the world. The man named Hector Elohim, would take the book with a promise of peace and salvation. Hartol paced the woods for hundreds of years in hope he had not betrayed his creators, deep down he prayed Hector Elohim was a true god who searched for a vessel on earth to deliver his promise of change.

MARY 1721

It was a bitter winters day the earth was hard and grey and the wind sang a somber tune, bringing hail and a vicious twist in a chilling gust, the little cottage stood on the side of the ancient wood, smoke funnelled from the chimney following the winds path, it swirled over the tree tops and trickled over the village, leaving only its aroma and a deeply sorry tale to follow. The cottage lay in stillness defeated by it sad news, the sister and brother huddled together, as the family grieved the loss of little Mary taken so suddenly by the fever. On the other side of the wood another cottage toiled in pain, a baby was born only to die in such a short time, two tragedies so close and so quickly, many would ask the question why. Sarah was little Mary's sister, she was only eight years old and could not bear to be inside a moment longer, the pain of loosing sweet little Mary was far to much for her to reconcile, how would she play and carry on, her little cot would be cold and empty without her sister by her side, always there just breathing gently with the smell of sweet lavender to calm her. Sarah thought of her funny little giggle and curious mind, how she loved the birds and flowers, as Sarah ran she thought of little Mary, her tears continued to fall, she ran and ran until she could barely breath in any more of the distasteful morning air. Sarah collapsed on the soft mossy woodland floor, she lay still and listened to the noises of birds and the rustling leaves, the black bird scratched and scraped next to her, scampering red squirrels ignored her sadness and bustled on by. Sarah then heard water so went to take a drink, amazed she found a pool so clear her reflection gazed back, for a moment she thought she saw someone in her looking glass of water, she turned to see just trees bracken and ferns, she thought she heard the sound of singing and decided it was just the gentle breeze fluttering the leaves. Sarah drank the water so clear she thought it must be safe, she then followed the stream that filled the crystal pool, it bought her to a wonderful waterfall that cascaded through the rocks, the place felt so magical. Sarah briefly forgot her grief as she explored the pretty Dell she marvelled at the dainty out of season flowers that grew in abundance, little violets, primroses, forget-me-nots and shiny bright celandines, like little stars shone amongst the rocks and foliage, Sarah daintily picked a tiny little posy for her Ma and started on her way back home, the woods were confusing though and the paths led in many ways, Sarah started to feel panic, she was lost in the spooky woods with many ghostly tales, she started to bolt and by chance and luck she bumped into a friendly face, a boy she had seen in Church, Sarah didn't know his name and declared abruptly that she needed desperately to get back home and had no way of knowing the way, the boy introduced himself as Tom the gamekeeper's son and said he knew the way, keeping very close Sarah followed, Tom walked fast and whistled like a bird, they didn't talk on their walk back to Sarah's cottage, both lost in their own thoughts, they instead listened to Tom's bird song and he shared his apple and scone, much to Sarah's delight, Sarah saw her cottage, she thanked Tom and ran, she waved back to him, but he had faded into the distance and all she could see was the woods at the end of the track. Sarah sneaked back into the cottage and wished she was back in the woods, she gave her Ma the posy who laid it beside little Mary, flowers had been put in her hair and she wore her best Sunday dress that used to be Sarah's. Sarah so bereft could only hide away. The next few days would remain to be agonising for everyone and Sarah had no chance to escape back to the woods and the pretty Dell, it engulfed her thoughts with its beauty and helped her cope each day, at night she would drift to sleep with her little baby brother Bobby snuffling by her side, she would dream of the crystal pool and playing in the flowers. Bobby's cries would wake her from her dreams, she would cuddle him gently and sing a lullaby to him. The days went quickly for Sarah, yet baby Bobby kept her busy and thankfully this gave her less time to think of the loss of little Mary, Sarah noticed Ma didn't cuddle, coo or even look at Bobby anymore. Papa said she needed time to be alone, so Sarah became Bobby's temporary Ma, Sarah did not feel any complaints towards her duty and considered it a joy, a responsibility that would help her ma get better and she hoped the day was soon.

TOMS APPLE 1721

Tom woke on the dreaded spring morning to wailing and tears, his bedroom was in the little attic that he shared with a few mice and his surly brother, who he disliked greatly, he was cruel and nasty and Tom secretly prayed for the day he would leave. Tom ran down the creaky stairs to find his Pa crying and his Ma swaying, the barely born baby had come into this world and only stayed for a few delicate breaths of life. Mother Darcey who saw to all the births in the village, gasped and tutted that the infant was not meant for this world, that the lord worked in mysterious ways, the baby Mary was meant for much better things than to walk on the path of a humble man. Tom became frustrated with her endless sermons and revelations, they were making things far worse, so he left quietly with tears stinging his eyes, by the back door his brother Guy stood leaning against the wall smoking, he spat the tobacco from his stained mouth and just looked at Tom with his piercing eyes, his scarred and cracked face for someone so young turned away, for once even Guy said nothing foul, Tom relieved went and let the chickens out and did some garden jobs for his Pa, although he was only eight he was expected to earn his keep, he collected the eggs and put them in the little porch, Guy thankfully had stomped off, he worked at the dusty stone mines further along the valley, a cruel and dangerous place, Tom hoped he would not have to work there ever, he prayed by shadowing his Pa, he to could become a game keeper, Tom loved the woods and birds and cared for nature, unlike Guy, he was thoughtless for anything living, Tom thought Guy was in the best place for him, smashing out rock with his burly friends who drank and got up to pranks and far worse. Tom hovered a little, then when he saw Mother Darcey go he went back into the cottage, to see if he could visit his Ma, his Pa ruffled his hair and patted him like a faithful dog, he said she was sleeping and is was best he left her, his Pa then gave him a note to take to Warliegh Manor, he was to tell them his Pa would be off work and Tom would feed the game and check the woods. So off Tom went released from the sadness in the house and elated his Pa trusted him with such a job, Tom got Buster from the shed, Buster was a terrier and had a lovely temperament, even though he looked very scary when he growled and barked at strangers, he was good at ratting and fetching, Tom threw him some food then they started out a cross the fields to the huge Manor house that loomed up from the slopes of the gentle valley, Tom found the butler John as instructed and past on his Pa's note, news had travelled fast and Tom heard Mother Darcey's irritating booming voice coming from the kitchens below, John looked sorry for Tom and asked him to wait, he came back with a bundle of food and sent him on his way with his condolences, Tom ran off with Buster at his side they went down into the woods and he set about feeding the game and filling water, he busily worked away checking everything was as it should be, Tom was worried he might see a poacher, his Pa carried a gun, he only had his pocket knife, Buster was growly but no match for a poachers dog, fortune was on his side though and no poachers were about, so he settled in the sunny glade and opened the bundle of food, his eyes lit up as he found a glazed meat pie, a bottle of ale, an apple and two scones, hungrily Tom ate the pie and drank the ale, the pie was the most delicious thing he had ever tasted, he decided to save one scone and the apple for later, Tom sat for longer than he realised with the soporific effect of the ale, slowly he stirred and checked the gates were all locked on the track to Claverton, so horses, carts and coaches couldn't use it as a byway, satisfied he had done his duties he started back towards home with some reluctance, he dragged his feet back with his head firmly down, as he rounded the narrow wooded path, to his shock a girl crashed straight into him, he knew immediately she was Sarah from the village, his Pa knew her family, she seemed quite distressed and finding she was lost, he started to guide her back to her home, Tom didn't really know what to say to a girl, so he decided instead of talking he would impress her and try to cheer up her sad face, with his brilliant bird song impressions, she seemed to like them and skipped along by his side. Tom had seen her in church and thought her the sweetest girl he had ever seen, he reached into his pocket and cut the apple in half with his knife, Sarah happily took her portion and gleamed, when he shared his scone she looked like he had given her a pearl, enjoying her presence, he regretted finding her neat cottage so soon, she mumbled thank you and the two parted company with just a smile, Tom looked back and waved but couldn't see Sarah, he felt bad because he felt happy, he thought of Mother Darcy's annoying words and thought what a wonderful day he had, on such a sad day and then Tom felt tears, he was thankful to his baby sister Mary he would never meet, he felt somehow Mother Darcy was truthful, because he sensed something different that day, he had the strangest feeling in the woods as though they spoke to him that all was going to be well and although sad, he had great hope for himself and for Sarah. When he got back home the cottage was quiet, Pa was sat with his brother his Uncle Thomas, while his wife Aunt Mable was busy cooking on the stove, when he walked in she ran to him and cuddled him, she told him to wash his hands outside and go see his Ma, Uncle Thomas gave him the complimentary hair ruffle with his glinting eyes, Tom went up the narrow steep staircase, his Ma sat up in bed with sweet tea and biscuits, she looked pale and sad, she managed a smile for Tom though, Tom sat on the bed next to her as gently as possible, he asked her where baby Mary had gone, his Ma gestured to the parlour, Tom held her hand and said he was sorry and sad, he told her about his day and how he thought baby Mary was looking out for him and how much he loved her even though he never met her, Tom told his Ma about the food and Sarah, she smiled and seemed happy with his tales, she fell asleep with a smile on her face, so Tom left her thinking things would be good from now on, baby Mary had their backs. Tom went up to his attic room hoping Guy would not be back yet, the little window was open that looked out onto the garden, Tom could still smell Guy's tobacco, he started to look around and realised something was strange all Guy's stuff had gone, not a trace was left of him. Tom ran downstairs to tell his Pa, his Pa nodded and said he just left, apparently he was joining some welsh men he had met, who were all off to Portsmouth to join one of Black Bart's ships, he said he was going to make his fortune. His Pa shrugged and Tom went back to his bedroom, thinking to himself about his brother joining a ships crewe and going out to sea, Tom knew he would probably never see him again, he tried hard not to feel smug as he pushed his little bed near the window and put the chair by it. Tom sat in the chair looking out of the window, no more nasty words or being thumped when he came home drunk, no more tobacco and stale ale smells, Guy was truly gone, he couldn't help but thank baby Mary she had bought him some luck, Tom wished desperately though that she had lived he would have loved a little sister, his trance was broken as his Pa called him downstairs, closing his little bedroom door, Tom looked back just one more time to check Guy was truly gone.

THE SABBATH 1721

The sabbath came and the day Sarah dreaded they would bury little Mary along with baby Mary, Tom's tiny sister who had only seen the world for wisp of a breath and her own precious sister who had come into the world like a curious playful lamb, at least Sarah thought she had felt the sun on her face and wind in her hair, tears streamed down Sarah's cheeks as she thought of her playful nature and pretty eyes, she would never see again, Sarah brushed her tears away and thought of the Dell and prayed that Mary could see it's beauty. The funerals were a somber affair and Sarah's Ma seemed in a trance, she looked pale and listless as if she had had her life sucked away from her, Sarah held baby Bobby and cooed his cries away, she saw Tom in church and smiled at him through her tears, he looked tired and seemed to try and comfort his Pa, his Ma was nowhere to be seen. Sarah worried for him more then herself, she had Bobby, Tom only had his older brother who had disappeared and was hard and unkind, his other brothers and sisters had left home for jobs or marriage a little like Sarah's, she had older sisters and a brother who all lived near by, she liked to visit them with her Ma and then her tears began again, because Mary wouldn't be there anymore. Sarah tried to focus hard on the hymns and the sermon, but the service was a blur, later standing out in the graveyard she felt slightly better with the stale smells and stuffiness gone, the adults all stood for ages talking and crying, as the children wandered off to potter around, Sarah found herself in a group of the village children, some her cousins, all of them were kind to her and they sat making daisy chains, while others played kicking pine cones around, Tom came and sat next to Sarah, they discussed with each other how they hadn't known of each others loss, the day they met by accident in the woods. Sarah asked Tom if he knew about the pool and Dell, he looked at her quizzically and they quickly agreed to go, no one would notice them slip away and the wake would go on for hours, Aunt Martha had baby Bobby so Sarah took her freedom whilst she could, the little church sat at the foot of the valley not far from Sarahs cottage, they cut across the meadow, Sarah thought hard which path she had taken once they entered the wood, as she stood starring at the different paths a black bird landed and flew back and forth as if to say you need to come this way, so they took the little over grown path and as they walked, Sarah remembered it was the way, still the black bird hopped in front flying and jumping, it seemed to lead the way, Tom laughed at its curious nature and how tame it seemed, both skipped along the path as if they had no cares in the world and the deeper into the wood they travelled, their thoughts of home and grief went further away, instead they admired their surroundings and enjoyed their new found freedom and friendship, eventually they arrived at the Dell and crystal pool, they both looked at the clear waters and saw their faces brightly reflecting back at them, again Sarah felt sure she saw something and turned to see nothing, Tom looked startled, he had seen another reflection, now they knew they were not alone, not afraid though they sat by the huge oak tree, Tom told Sarah stories of the woodland that his Grandpa had told him, the woods were magical and had spirits and ghosts, for centuries people had reported sightings of a girl dressed in white on the track and others saw a white stag in the depths of the forest, ancient tales were told of the weather suddenly changing to a storm in anger or the birds stopping their song, others said magical plants grew and some said that there were hidden waters that made you immortal, Sarah didn't know what that meant and hoped it was not bad, as she had drunk quite a lot, then Tom got up and went to the water cupping some in his hand, he thirstily drank it, then called to the woods he would live forever, Sarah giggling copied him, understanding what the word immortal meant, with some relief, she looked thankfully at Tom knowing he understood she had not known the meaning of immortal, they ran and skipped by the stream and dangled their hands in the icy waterfall that cascaded musically over the rocks, they wandered around the Dell and marvelled at its beauty, Tom said he thought the legends were true, the wood was magical as plants grew that would not normally bud until later in the following spring and they both agreed the breeze sounded like music in the trees, all the time though they felt watched by something or someone, that feeling didn't leave them until later when they running across the meadows to the Manor, where the wake had been arranged, as both Sarah and Tom's Pa's and Ma's worked there, they joined the wake in the huge tithe barn, trestle tables were laden with home baked food and jugs of ale, Tom and Sarah went to grab as much as they could and sat under the table as though they had been there the whole time, both full to the brim they lay down and watched peoples feet pass them by, Sarah then heard Martha calling her name, she smiled at Tom and scurried off. Baby Bobby was handed over to her, she happily cuddled him and smelt his lavender hair, Sarah felt another punch of sadness for their loss, maybe though the spirits in the woods had played their magic on her mind, as inside she felt a happiness that was new and a deep feeling something was different that was good and true.

A BRIDGE IN THE WOODS 1643

Sir Waller woke early pleased with his previous days work, he rose surrounded by damp from the heavy morning dew, the watery sun sleepily showed itself through whispery clouds and the birds chorus grew, his bridge constructed over the narrow part of the river stood ready for their conquest, in the name of his King he would battle with the on coming Roundheads in hope to help ease the inevitable battle at Landsdowne, his men woke in turn and with little word they began to ready both themselves and their horses, each ate their potage and stale bread, they fed and watered the horses and hid any trace of their over night camp and morning activities, each man horse and weapon crossed the rackety bridge, recovering it with branches and felled trees making sure their escape was hidden as not to help the enemy. The small yet well equipped and skilled army entered the thick woodland and struggled through the deep thickets, they headed for a track, they knew the Roundheads would be forced to take, their path was small and only used by dear and fox, the huge war horses smashed through the foliage and fauna. Waller was a ruthless knight a warrior who felt no fear, yet he could not help feeling they were being closely watched, he had felt the same ever since they had arrived in the valley of woods, it was the strangest feeling he felt a feeling he did not like, he convinced his mind maybe a local watched with curiosity, though he did not investigate, the day grew more eerie and as they trod the ancient paths not usually passed by man and horse, Waller and his men felt a sense of something greater than a curious eye, the morning was still mild and calm, with glimpses of sun through the deep canopy above, yet from nowhere a ferocious and wild storm suddenly started, the wind howled and the wood darkened, driving rain found them through the trees and as they positioned themselves in the glade, ready to ambush, the skies grumble and clouds gathered so loud was the thunder that they struggled to hear the on coming horses hooves, lightning flashed above the canopy of trees and each man struggled to hold the horses calm, their ambush was becoming impossible, fearless and brave they stood their ground and charged at the oncoming army, each side confused by the weather fought badly, with poor vision and any sense of sound, as the ear splitting thunder cracked above, the sally through the woods became impossible and Wallers men drove on eventually loosing sight and sound of their victims, many laid dead on the woodland floor. Still the storm prevailed sending Waller and his men away, they doubled back afraid to go forward finding their way to the bridge to escape back over into Claverton and join the rest of the army in Landsdowne, their bridge though lay in ruins from the storm so they turned back and journeyed up into the Brown Folly Woods, Waller felt uneasy so skirted back the long way around, the storm grew again and as they tried to get up onto the track torrents of water drove them away, they broke to the hill in hope they could see a clear way that was safe and as Waller looked back through the dusk, he saw a white stag rearing in the woods as is if in victory, puzzled Waller and his men continued, the darkness started to grow afraid now they would be ambushed, they rode on a long track on the other side of the valley the storm had eased and the more seasonal gentle winds replaced the skies, all wet and exhausted the horses trudged on with riders to fearful to stop, as they continued the army of men did not know if they dreamt or were haunted that night, for each saw the vision of a girl running across the track in white, she screamed like a banshee and captured each soldiers eye the horses reared and bolted causing chaos and injury, Waller prayed for the night to end and eventually he and his few men found shelter and peace by a spring far from the woods at Farleigh, a night none would like to repeat. Defeated that night they told the story often of the strange woods with its mystical weather and ghosts. Over the years the stories would grow and travellers would fear the paths and go many miles to avoid the torments of the ghosts of Brown Folly Woods.

LACEY 1386

Lacey was eight years old she had been taken in by the monks when she was only four years old, her Ma and Pa had drowned whilst escaping at sea, Lacey didn't remember much of the fateful night other than a dreadful fear and a terrifying coldness, she now knew was her near death. The monastery became her silent prison with hard work, strict rules and cold beds, the rats came at night and scuttled around taking what they could, Lacey dreamt of escaping from the walls she was trapped in, the master was nasty and not what you would think from a man of god, crooked in mind and body he took what he could from the rich and treated the destitute like slaves, with just enough food to survive, thankfully many of the monks were kind and generous to the orphans, they taught them well and spared them many chores, they disliked their Abbot but could only make a wrong right by helping with secret food and kindness, they gave aid when someone was taken ill, although the infirmary in the monastery was not a good place to end up, Lacey had seen very few make it out alive, her little friend Betsy had only gone in with a few spots and was never seen again, ever since then Lacey had been lonely and sad. Lacey would often try and find brother Hugh he was rounded fellow, with a cheery generous nature, he always had something to eat tucked in his habit, brother Hugh was in charge of the masonic garden, when the horrible Abbot brother John was away he was in charge of the monastery and it became a happier and more lenient place, sadly Abbot John would always return though, brother Hugh had grown a soft spot for little Lacey, she was bright and funny, he would start to give her lessons on useful talents that may help her in life, so when ever possible he would show her how to sew and do different stitches, he also taught her how to weave the willow and reeds that they harvested from the river banks, he even showed her how to count with sticks, at first she could see no point in knowing how many sticks there were, until he secretly showed her the counting house, with groats he was able to demonstrate to her, how much she was owed for her woven basket and how she would know if she had been paid fairly, Lacey after that demonstration started to count everything, brother Hugh laughed at her appetite for learning, he was very pleased with her progress and felt certain she would benefit in service somewhere else, knowing the Abbot would never help her further than becoming a serf, so brother Hugh took it upon himself to source a position for at her at Farleigh Castle, intending her to become a ladies maid. Lacey had prayed for the day she could escape although to what or where she had no clue, her life was one of uncertainty. One day she was relieved from her duties of scrubbing the food hall floor and was asked to go to the front, she was without word taken in a carriage to a huge castle, she was scrubbed like a dog in the freezing yard and then dressed in white crisp clothes, she was taken to the kitchens bellowing away in the depths of the castle. Lacey was told she would be trained first in laundry, to Lacey she was now just a washer serf, she had escaped one trap for a crisp clean capture instead. Lacey felt sad she had not been able to say goodbye to brother Hugh and some of the others, she knew she was not to far from the Abbey, so maybe one day she would pay a visit to them, this thought kept her from crying, Lacey did not like the castle it was worst than the Abbey with drafts, rats the size of wild cats and horse manure everywhere, she slept in a cot near an old hag, who smelt dreadful and snored the night away, the hag named Ibb was always cross and a thief, after week of insufferable behaviour, Lacey relocated herself to the horses barn outside, she found a well tempered horse she named Isope; after the fables she had heard in the monastery; when Isope had finished eating his hay, she would snuggle up in his rack away from harm, the stall felt warm and safe, Lacey began to enjoy her evenings and even Isope was pleased to see her, as she always went to the trouble of finding them both a carrot to munch on. Lacey also made a friend with a boy of her age called Billy, he was funny and loved to act the jester. Billy worked in the horses barn and knew that Lacey slept in the stall, he promised to keep her secret and the two became very enterprising friends, Lacey showed Billy how to count and weave, he was thrilled and said he felt like a wizard. Lacey laughed and said he was more like scarecrow with straw stuck out of his hat and tunic, Billy didn't mind her teasing, he was happy to have a clever friend, Billy collected reeds on morning of the Sabbath, he hid them well in the barn and at night they would both weave away, then Lacey on her afternoon off, would take them to the castle market and sell them for a groat each, it was not long before they had saved twenty whole groats, hidden well in Isope's stall, at night they counted them in rows. One night they both agreed they should run, if someone found their purse, they would be accused of stealing and hung or worse. Lacey and Billy knew it was now far too dangerous for them to stay, so they planned to run away as soon as possible. Lacey cried when saying goodbye to Isope, she hugged his huge neck and kissed him goodbye, Billy grabbed hold of her and in darkness they crept away, they would walk all night to get far enough from Farleigh castle, Lacey thought it best to walk away from the larger settlement, where the Abbey was with the spring waters and walk towards the little town on the river, when the morning dawn came they hid in a tiny church just above the huge river, its mellow carved stone protected them through the day, hidden behind a decorative stone alter they patiently waited and slept, the little monastic church was quiet that day once a mortuary for saint Edward the Martyr, the present nuns took prayer and any that glimpsed the waif like bodies, pretended not to, believing the lord would sort their sleeping guests in his own way. Lacey and Billy stirred with aching backs and limbs, by the altar a jug of milk and loaf of bread had been left, hungrily they ate and drank, in place of the milk jug they left a groat and once again persevered with their great escape, cold and wet from the evening drizzle they followed the woodland paths, hidden from view they skirted along on the east side with the river below, that meander through the valley in the direction of the Abbey, the woodland was very thick and gave them endless places to hide, by the time dawn was just beginning to arrive, Lacey and Billy were deep in the ancient woods far from any settlements, paths or tracks, they found a huge old oak tree and climbed up into it, setting in its cradling branches and hidden by leaves Billy and Lacey fell fast asleep.

BROWN FOLLY WOODS 1386

The ancient woods stretched for miles, each tree was enormous, with branches that had incredible huge spans, the soft woodland floor would often stay dry in the rain, as the canopies were so thick, water would trickle to find the roots, springs popped up with gushing clear waters, in the deepest part of the wood a waterfall of crystal waters cascaded over the lime stone rocks and fell into a natural stone basin, the waters so clear and stone so mellow, it created a glistening magical pool. The wood was full of creatures from the smallest mouse to the largest stag, the creatures would take waters from the special spring with the glistening crystal flow and life was eternal and good. One such creature was Hartol his name was given by the Gods to the pure white and noble stag, he had flowing white fur and his antlers glistened, Hartol ruled the woods and was loved by all, he was powerful and protected his empire with pride, for centuries all lived in peace and life's balance was how it should be. This would not last forever though and man would come along toiling, fighting and hunting, as warned by the Gods. Hartol needed to always be on his guard, to watch and be strong, he patrolled his woods daily and had spies in every part, no man could reach their Dell or all their hope was gone, for centuries they battled off many wandering souls and had clashes with armies and arriving settlements, each time though Hartol pushed them far away in fear, they all left his domain and did not return. Hartol was worried though so many more humans had started to come through the woods and cause damage, he feared he could not always protect the Dell and Brown Folly Woods, he desperately needed a plan and he passed through the waterfall to another time long ago to speak with the Gods and Star Gazers he spoke to Princess Hehet who saw his concern, she agreed they needed to become more defensive and intervene. He left Hehet as she mutter and mumbled her thoughts that formed her cunning plans. Convinced he had influenced the Gods he felt some satisfaction, he still needed to carry out his part of the plan and by chance one late summers evening he saw an intriguing gentle looking pair come his way, he would normally drive even little humans away, this enchanting pair though seemed different, they were clad in white and looked like angels, both quiet and gentle they did no harm but instead did good, he watched them from a far and saw their kindness and respect, Hartol decided to let them further than any had travelled before into his domain, he needed to know how they would react to his world, Hartol knew he needed human help and these humans he felt sure could help with their gentle ways, he watched them thin the willow with care and weave their wonderful nest, he saw them making food from fruits fallen to the floor and fish for just enough, unlike their relations they were not greedy or destructive, the morning they arrived by chance into the Dell, he witnessed their reaction as they saw the Dell and stunning crystal pool, they danced with joy and did no harm, they did not even sip the precious waters, giddy they ran back to their part of the woods. Hartol knew they would visit again and again how could they not resist its beauty, one day soon he hoped he would greet them and ask them somehow for their help in his part. So the plan had begun the Gods were already spinning a tale and it was not by chance the two angels had met, or that others would soon become enthralled in their quest.

FARLIEGH HUNGERFORD CASTLE 1386

The castle stood as a fortress and powerful reminder of its wealth and brutal rights of the land, local peasants would witness their village destroyed, where small huts once stood a deer park was to be created, tree felling had begun, the process was a painful reminder for many, who now endured service to the castle for survival. Sir Thomas Hungerford was a domineering lord of his land and had powers from his role in government and ties with other wealthy and influential leaders including the King. His only surviving son Walter would inherit his kingdom a knight himself, the castle he hoped would continue to hold its own dominance for many years to come, much to its serfs disappointment. The imposing castles had stunning views over the rolling valley, ancient woodland and clear waters of the river, its towers looked out onto their tranquil setting, ironically such breath taking beauty, held a sinister truth of death and torture within the castle walls, serfs were sworn to secrecy and their fear would keep their tongues quiet, to leave was not an option ever unless by death. The discovery of two missing serfs was slow on the morning of the sabbath, the castle rouse later that morning after huge celebrations, they had heard news of a win in the battle of the clans in Scotland, for England the best clan had won politically, not many understood yet rejoiced because they felt they should. The horses had all been let out to the fields to graze, with no battles for both knights and horses there was rest on the sabbath, other than serving food. It was not until the banquet was served and the serfs were set to eat in the kitchen that the two places were visibly empty and even then they laughed, joking maybe they were sweet on each other. Everyone turned a blind eye, there were more important things and to waste a good meal with fine mead was not an option. Much was drunk and the discovery of the missing serfs would extend to the next morning, with doubt they were really gone, the alarm was not raised, an agreement of secrecy and lies, each afraid for their own lives, the search unfolded and not a trace of the young serfs could be found, a rumour was started that they had seen to young serfs swimming in the river, it was then assumed they had both drowned, such young serfs would never have the intelligence or bravery to run away. Little effort was made to find their bodies and few cared of their absence they were easily replaced, although both the stable head and washer woman felt the loss of their gentle ways and good work, Billy had away with horses like no other and Lacey was sweet and kind. Brother Hugh would visit the castle some time later that week and to hear the sad news was more than he could bare, he thought of her sweetness and bright mind, brother Hugh hid his grief though and only later whilst riding back to the priory, did he allow his tears to fall, once he had regained his composure, Hugh remembered something of importance and hope, Lacey would not swim she would not go near water, her parents were drowned and she was close to death, although she remembered little, he had seen her whine and run from the river many times. Where Lacey and the stable boy were he had no clue, Hugh strongly felt it was not the tangled weeds and river bed though, he prayed they were safe and kept his thoughts to himself. His plan for her to become a ladies maid though had sadly fallen through.

SOMETHING ABOUT MARY 1721

Sarah finished her chores and seeing the day was beautiful; whilst pegging out the washing with difficulty on her wobbly stool; she decided to take baby Bobby out for a walk. Her Pa was gardening at the Manor and her Ma although still sickly had also gone back to service, she was a cook in the kitchens of the Manor house. Sarah was often now left alone with Bobby, she still did not complain and was glad of his company, she found the little hand cart; her Pa had made and used for collecting, wood, apples and other oddities; Sarah put Bobby's cradle in to it deciding he was far to heavy to carry and off she trundled, with little Bobby babbling happily, the sun felt warm and Sarah was glad to reach the shade of the wood, hot from pushing and pulling the cart, she decided to take the top path that she had worked out would lead her to Tom's cottage, his cottage sat on the edge of the woods and was very similar to Sarah's only with more land. The sun streamed through trees and scents filled the breeze, the day had a happy feel to it and Sarah felt elated. She had taken up the habit of talking to Mary, as though she was by her side, so as she stumbled along the path she chatted away about all her worries and hopes, she talked about the things she saw and felt, Sarah found great comfort in chattering to her lost sister Mary, she hoped no-one saw her, although maybe they would think she talked to her baby brother, Bobby no doubt thought she was. Sarah decided to cut the corner off the path by going through the wood, she struggled with the cart, determined though she carried on and reached the path well trodden by deer and foxes, it was then Sarah glimpsed the stag as white a snow and both stood still as stone staring at one another, the stag then turned and disappeared into the depths of the wood thicket. Sarah was amazed never had she seen anything so beautiful transfixed to the spot in hope it would return, Sarah talked still out a loud describing the wonder she had just seen, as if by doing this she would record the wonderful sight forever and a little voice by her side told her not to tell anyone else, at first Sarah thought it was her own imagination, or even her own words, then she saw her as plain as the sky was blue, little Mary stood there, shocked by her apparition, Sarah started to walk and the little ghost skipped along beside her chattering away about her knew friends in the woods and how much fun she had every day, Sarah started to relax and enjoy this knew phenomenon and chatted back as though it was the most normal thing in the world, she partly thought it was just her imagination and then she would see Mary skip and jump and she felt sure it was real, as she left the wooded path that came out near Toms cottage, Mary faded away and Sarah realised quickly the woods were the key to her sister's ghost, Sarah asked questions in her mind, did her little spirit follow her that day, could something magical have happened, Sarah still deep in thought hardly noticed she was at the door of Tom's home and then felt a sudden panic of realisation, she didn't know what she was going to say. Tom's dog Buster came running around the garden barking and growling, she quickly grabbed the giggling Bobby holding him close, Buster just wagged his tale, as Tom came running not far from behind, he grinned pleased to see her and bid her to follow him, Sarah grabbed the jar of milk in the cart and dutifully followed, Tom was busy gardening for his Pa they had a huge vegetable patch that he was busy weeding and mulching, Sarah knew lots about gardening from her own Pa, so lying the now sleeping Bobby down she set about helping him weed. Sarah decided to tell Tom about the white stag she knew she could trust him, although she would keep the something about Mary quiet, in fear Tom would think she had gone completely barmy. Tom was so excited she had seen the white stag and he believed her completely, much to her relief. He told her there were many folk tales about the white stag and ghostly sightings in Brown Folly Woods, he said his Pa once saw a ghostly figure of a girl on the track, Sarah winced she found it all a little creepy, especially as she knew now it was true, ghosts did exist. They both finished off the vegetable patch, fed Bobby and decided to see if they could see the stag again, Sarah was sure he lived near the crystal pool and Dell. Tom helped with the cart nether of them thought of the time, with Bobby and Buster by their side though they had no need, Tom had worked out another way to the Dell so they walked across the open meadows for a little before entering the wood, it was very thick and hard to get through especially with a cart, with some effort though they managed by pulling, pushing and lugging, eventually they broke through the thicket, with a few scratches and scrapes, as they journeyed deeper into the wood it started to go very still and the only sound that could be heard was the musical swish of the trees. Tom and Sarah were a little afraid, they carried on though feeling they would not be harmed, the wood was giving up all its secrets and both fauna, flora and creatures glistened with a white glow and each carried on its business with no regard for their visitors, through the trees they heard the sound of galloping and before them stood the white stag. The stag lifted his head up and down and they were sure he spoke and then to their disbelief a young girl appeared, no older than eight, she was all in white and had the palest complexion and silver hair she had the sweetest smile and spoke how Sarah imagined an angel to speak, her voice sang the words of greetings and help. The ghostly figure introduced herself as Lacey as she danced around, she made them promise to keep their secret and told them the legend of Hartol the white stag and how they feared the tree cutters would encroach on their magical world. They had watched Tom and his father and seen they took care of Brown Folly Woods well, Lacey asked if they could help. Tom was uncertain what he could do he was just a simple boy, Lacey encouraged him, saying, they just needed them to agree all would be explained. Tom was feeling quite taken a back by all this and asked Sarah what she thought, Sarah was sometimes braver than Tom; his Pa would say she had a fire in her heart and was plucky for a lass; in the branches Sarah saw little Mary hiding from Tom with a ghostly boy, her mind reeled as to what was going on and if she dreamed this strange day, baby Bobby broke her thoughts as he giggled at the white rabbits as they bounced along the mossy floor, Sarah just thought quickly, that yes they should do everything they could to save this precious world, however strange she felt. Tom found his voice seeing Sarah's encouraging smile, Tom didn't know what they asked of him, he knew though he was true to the woods and nature and agreed to do all he could to help, giving his word and a gentle stroke of affection to the wonderful white stag named Hartol, they followed a small possession to the crystal pool, strange stunning blue lights shone from the pool and waterfall, Sarah glimpsed a strange woman through the waterfall their gazes locked for a second or two, then she was gone, Sarah kept looking the spectre, the image although no longer there lingered on and left Sarah feeling haunted. Tom didn't see the strange figure Sarah had described, he felt her fear though and held her hand, Tom started to believe that the Dell had some huge reason and was far more than just Brown Folly Wood and Warliegh Manor and the other estates of the land, this was some ancient world that fought to keep things as they were. Lacey broke his thoughts by introducing him to Billy, who immediately gave Tom and Sarah each a rosy red apple and joked that they would fall asleep for a thousand years, Lacey tutted at him as he continued to act the fool, Tom and Sarah laughed at Billy immediately liking his quirky ways, Sarah stayed close to Toms side and reached out for little Mary to join them, she shyly came down and sat with them on the mossy floor, Tom shocked beyond belief just stared at her while the others talked, soon a gathering grew and the forest animals, ghosts and the living sat to discuss the joy of the wonderful wood. Sarah felt more than surreal that afternoon, she felt as though something strange happened to her, not only did she feel an out of body experience, she also felt different it was as though she was two people, never could she explain this, not even to Tom.

BACK IN TIME FOR TEA 1721

Tom and Sarah left the wood that afternoon saying good bye to everyone, little Mary stayed happily with Lacey and Billy, making Sarah feel a little better leaving her, they were worried they would be very late, but discovered that not much time had passed at all, this strange world they had stumbled upon seemed to slow the days, while the world around it moved on quickly regardless. Tom and Sarah talked like never before on their walk home and agreed no soul should ever no about what they had found and seen, they had a pact and for some reason it felt huge, they were in the biggest escapade they could ever imagine. Tom helped Sarah back to the cottage and helped her with her chores he then ran home himself, when Tom had gone Sarah bathed Bobby in the tin bath by the fire, she put him in his bedtime clothes and lay him in the cot, exhausted Bobby slept flat out with his little arms and legs spread out, Sarah kissed him gently on the forehead and then went to the loft to find Mary's box, as she was sort of still around, she could have her favourite rag doll, Aunty Bess had made for her when she was born, they both had one each and they called them Bessie and Bess, Sarah looked at Mary's meagre little box, all that was left of her in the house, she felt sad and was not sure how to cope, with her little Mary as a ghost in the wood, for some reason, Mary seemed brimming with happiness as if she was unaware she was a ghost and what ever Sarah thought of Lacey and Billy they were kind to little Mary and seemed to have endless fun, even though they were ghosts, Sarah felt very confused and she grieved her loss for some reason a little more than before, she would take her the doll Bess and try to feel happy for her sister's fate, maybe it was meant to be, maybe little Mary also had a calling for greater things and was needed else where.

WILD THYME AND POTATOES

After their woodland adventure, Tom had left Sarah and ran back home worried his Ma would be back, he didn't like to think of her coming home to an empty house, she was still distraught and very pale, Tom knew she struggled more than she said, he thought about Mary, Sarah's sister in the woods, it was a strange business the whole thing and he felt unsettled and confused, Tom had always thought to himself baby Mary was a lucky charm and something happened that day, the day they lost the two Mary's, something very sad but also something greater, that Tom didn't quite understand, he now truly believed something was happening, something he could not explain. Tom saw his Ma walking along the lane towards the cottage, he quickly ran and joined her, hugging her and taking her hand he listened to her news from the Manor, she wasn't happy they had taken on a new young girl, who seemed far to confident and spelt trouble with her cocky way, her name was Isla and she came from an orphanage in town, she knew to much and Tom's Ma said she wouldn't put it past her to be light fingered, this Tom knew meant his Ma thought she was a thief, this was bad for all of the staff, if one thing went missing they were all under suspicion. His Ma stopped grumbling and asked him of his day, he just told his Ma about the chores and going for a walk and helping Sarah with Bobby, she smiled and said he was a good lad and Sarah's Ma was a lucky woman to have a daughter as good as gold like Sarah, she squeezed his hand and said it was special they were friends, especially as they both lost a Mary. Tom

smiled up at his Ma, but she was gone again into herself. Tom
wished he could tell her about the white stag, Lacey, Billy and
Mary, he wanted to make her happy, he knew though she would
not believe him and only become more upset. Tom went quiet and
began to miss the easy jolly company of Sarah, she was always so
generous with her kindness and good humour, Tom took himself
to garden to find wild thyme and some potatoes, knowing that
they were his Ma's favourite, the wind had gathered up, it paced
and howled around the valley like a wrathful wretch searching
out it's prey, he shuddered to himself and headed for the back
door, with relief he heard his Pa whistle as he came home, Tom ran
back out to great him, his Pa did the affectionate hair ruffle and
went with him to check on his vegetable garden progress, pleased
he patted him. Tom hesitantly asked him about the white stag and
tales of the woods, his Pa looked over to the woods and Tom
thought he was about embark on a wonderful tale, yet he just tutted and said they would keep for another time and he walked with
his head down towards the cottage, it seemed to Tom with reluctance, as though he walked in thick deep mud, Tom had noticed
his Ma and Pa didn't talk or laugh much any more, things were all
so tense, he hoped in time it would change, his Ma though was so
grumpy with his Pa, it was as though she blamed him for Mary
dying, she didn't go to church any more and wouldn't let the vicar
in to talk, despite the poor chaps attempts, whatever anyone said
they couldn't help his Ma, Tom thought she was cross and bitter
with the whole world, he was the only one she would give a smile
or a kind word to these days. Maybe one day she would change
back, for now though he had to keeping thinking how he could
help her. Tom made himself think of the Dell and helping them,
maybe in some way this would help his Ma and if little Mary was a
ghost he now believed anything could happen.

BROTHER HUGH 1376

Brother Hugh was fourteen years old he sat with his head down in prayer in the huge cathedral, his home and place of study. Hugh had arrived at Canterbury cathedral as a baby orphaned and left for dead, the monks had taken him in and his life from that day on was to serve God, the cathedral was full that day a funeral took place for Prince Edward known as the Black Prince, a noble knight who had won many battles in his time on earth. Hugh had attended many funerals this though was huge, many came to pay their respects and the service continued for many hours, Hugh felt guilty but he was glad when he could finally escape and attend to his chores, bored by the endless rituals and affairs, he often wished he could break free from his habit and cross, he had no clue though what he would do and how he would live, so afraid to stray of the path he stayed. Hugh finished of tending to his herbs and vegetables the season was nearly over and his last crop of potatoes would soon be ready to pull, deep in thought he wandered around the walled garden pulling any weeds as he went, startled he heard and saw something in the large bay bush, Hugh summoned up his courage and made a closer inspection, he saw little droplets of blood around the bush and he lifted the thickly leaved branch, Hugh then got the shock of his life, trying to hide and quite defenceless crouched a strange creature half human, half deer, Hugh startled fell back onto the path, he quickly composed himself, realising the creature was in pain and loosing blood, he offered the strange being his help, the creature shyly obliged, showing the deep cut on her leg, Hugh quickly ran to his shed and found a clean bowl and cloth he had for washing, he filled it with water and returned to his strange patient, he bathed the wound and rapped it

tightly in cloth, he had seen them do this in the infirmary so knew
it would stop the blood, Hugh then went to the back of the garden
and picked some nettles he crushed them into a pulp with some
water and then placed them on the bandage above the wound and
wrapped some more fabric around, he knew the nettles would
help heel and clean the wound, he then gave his patient water and
apples from the barrel, then Hugh had to decide what to do, heavy
rain was on its way and his stranger would most definitely need
shelter, without word he picked up the Faun and carried her to his
shed, at first she was trembling but he soothed her as he would a
rabbit found in a trap, Hugh had over the years made his shed
comfortable, no one ever came this way, other than the young lads
who helped him at the busy times of the year, so although it was a
penance he had a small bed in there made from straw and sack, he
lay the injured Faun on the bed and sat watching her for a while, as
she drifted off to sleep, her huge deer like eyes closed and she
snuffled like an animal, Hugh was intrigued as to how and earth
she had found herself in the garden, he worried it was something
evil that had harmed her and was fearful for her that it would
come looking, knowing a hunter would never give up this prize
easily. Hugh heard the bells ringing for evening prayer, he locked
the shed door and ran back hoping he would not be late. After
prayer Hugh hesitated and decided it was best to leave the Faun
that night, undisturbed he hoped she would sleep, Hugh rouse
very early and went to collect some oats from the kitchen sacks, he
nervously walked towards the little shed and opened the door
with hesitation afraid she may be dead, he was relief to see her still
lying but awake, he offered the oats and more apples and water
then changed the dressing and went for more nettles, again he ap-
plied them pleased with closing of the wound, Hugh chatted away
to his stranger, unsure if she understood and to his complete surprise she answered one of his indirect questions, the Faun had a
voice and her name was Arrietta, she came from woods far away
and had been captured by a cruel man and hidden in his grain
stall, she escaped and cut her leg badly in doing so, big tears rolled
down her face, she said she thought her family were dead, Hugh

comforted her a best he could and promised to help her, she thanked him for his kindness and hung her head in grief, Hugh was a positive person by nature and carried on chatting to her, trying to cheer her up. How he could help her though he was not sure. Fate had a funny way of being, for by chance later that day Hugh was called to the Abbot, Brother James was a kind man and was found of Hugh, he however felt although he was happy with his garden, he should expand his mind a little for someone his age, he had had a visit from the Abbot of the south west monastery in Bath, he sought an apprentice in a new herb garden with different species bought from abroad, it was perfect for Hugh and as the Abbot was here for the funeral, he could interview him and decide if he was the monk for the job. Brother Hugh had the situation explained to him and was comforted by the Abbot James, promising him he could come back if he was unhappy, brother Hugh immediately disliked the Abbot John of Bath, he was sharp tongued with an eerie unkindness about him, his eye's reminded Hugh of an eagle ready to attack his kill, he talked in an arrogant manner and seemed convinced that Hugh would take the job and be so thankful for this wonderful opportunity, brother Hugh was not sure, he knew it was a golden opportunity, it took him away though from everything and everyone he had known all his life, Hugh was lost in thought as his life passed in front of him, he felt lucky he had been so well cared for by the monks, he did not listen to the Abbot John's constant ramblings about how wonderful Bath was, Hugh's attention though snapped back to the conversation, when the Abbot John stated that he would first have to collect a delivery, that had travelled down from the docks at Hull, the arrangement was to meet in Dorchester On Thames after collecting a small parcel from Oxford and prior to that Dunstable priory, he was given all the details and would be supplied with funds for a horse and cart. Hugh was instructed he would leave the following week alone, Hugh felt both panic and freedom and also the wonderful realisation that he had away of smuggling Arrietta back to her home, over joyed at this thought he enthusiastically accepted the job, much to both of the Abbots surprise, so it was agreed money and paper work with instructions were exchanged, the interview was over, excused by the Abbot, Hugh went to tell Arrietta the good news, her huge eyes brimmed with tears of relief and thanks, she knew that this was a big thing for Hugh and that he did it for her freedom and safety and not for his own gains. Arrietta stayed well hidden in his garden hut, she had the odd little walk around the walled garden, when the coast was clear in the early evenings, Hugh spent his time preparing and packing his meagre belongings, he found a solid pony and trap from the local black smiths, who was happy to sell them both for a profit. The pony was a sturdy number, he called him Struddle after a lovely long apple pie Brother Hans would often make, Struddle was golden and white with a long flowing mane and tail, with feathers on his legs, he had him well shod in the agreement and the simple wooden cart was fixed and the wheels tightened, proud of his accomplishment Hugh went to find Abbot James, to ask if he could leave earlier, saying he wished for a little time to take in the wonders of Oxford and especially to see more of the priory of St Frideswide, Abbot James agreed with open arms and said he would arrange for lodgings and a stable, Hugh spent the rest of the day saying his goodbyes to the other monks, he no longer felt sad but excited and he knew one day he would be back if only to visit. The Abbot James had said life was to short to spend on one vegetable patch alone, he had encouraged him to go out into the world and learn, he also told Hugh to be true to himself and follow the path he was taken upon, Hugh never understood what he really meant until a time a little later in his life, when he would realise the Abbot James pushed him to something far greater than a garden of continental herbs. The next morning Hugh woke at dawn, he packed up the cart carefully placing the straw and sacks, with Arrietta hidden beneath, Hugh and Struddle trundled out of Canterbury he headed out on the river path towards Dunstable Priory, with hope to make it by night fall.

THE BLACK PRINCE 1376

The day the Black Prince died he took an amazing secret to the grave and for many this was a great blessing. Edward known as the Black Prince, was a well regarded son of King Richard, who showed bravery and skills in war, he had won many battles in the hundred year war between France and England, a negotiator and fierce leader, he was the meaning of chivalry. It was sad his life ended with an all to the common illness of dysentery, after all his battles and bravery. Edward had encountered something even beyond his comprehension, whilst traveling back from a parliamentary discussion in Bristol, he had become lost and found himself in a huge ancient wood that stretched far a cross the south west, he had with him a small army of men for protection, eventually they found the Bath monastery and its hospitality with fine food and wines, the Black Prince decided to stay a little longer intrigued by the woodland and he tarried around the woods game hunting for sport, famous for its abundance in deer and other game, on his final day the Prince enjoyed his last hunt and they became involved in an exhilarating chase, they had wounded one of the deers in a heard, yet still it ran, Edward was a fierce knight, he could be a reasonable man though and would rather the wretched animal was killed and not left to die in a sorrowful way, he also wanted his trophy of antlers for his walls. The chase however became a battle of whits and other forces blocked their way, confused and not a man to be defeated he carried on beyond that day and into the next, it was early that morning at dusk that Edward glimpsed his prey alone, on foot he crept with his arrow set, he hit the stag to the ground as it fell a calf ran to its side, Edward was upon them quickly and what he saw was incredible both stag and calf were half human, half deer and he knew these were just two of the heard that they chased, realising the stag was huge and feeling strangely unsafe, Edward stole the young calf keeping its head hidden from the others he travelled back with it over his saddle, the creature lay as if it was dead, on arriving back in Canterbury the prince roughly untied it and callously threw it in his grain stall, he did not care wether it lived or died it was his proof that a strange army of half human, half deer roamed his Kings land and that they must be hunted and killed, he felt they could only be the creation of some evil. Edward felt poorly that evening, he thought he was just exhausted and took to his bed, within hours he was delirious and by day break he lay dead, with the creature locked and hidden away, without word to another soul. His proof of devilment and a strange being would never be shared with another human, that was until brother Hugh found the Black Princes's victim in his bay bush. Arrietta had been thrown into Edwards disused grain stall with the doors locked, she spent two days and nights shivering with fear, she thought of her beloved Brown Folly Woods and her family herd so far away, Arrietta was young though and found her strength, she searched the old store for any chance of escape, Arrietta tired, was ready to give up her prison seemed to have no escape, she lay curled tightly in a ball as her tears fell, her attention was taken by a curious rat who sniffed at her then scattered off on his business, showing Arrietta a sizeable hole in the store, she had missed, quickly she got up and set to work, Arrietta kicked and kicked at the rotten wood, for hours she kept going and eventually exhausted she cracked open a gap big enough to slip through, injured from her kicking she limped for hours and by chance found the safety of the walls and garden full of food, Arrietta nibbled on the tasty herbs knowing they would help her heal, she then rested in the bush, praying her leg would mend itself. Arrietta knew the Gods were looking out for her that night, something drove her to the safety of the gardens and the kindness of her saviour clad in brown robes.

THE FAUNS AND SALLY 1376

Artu and Adelleta stood on the hill looking over the ancient woods, the herd stood close behind, they searched for their lost Faun, Arrietta had now been missing for over a week since the attack of the war man, Artu himself had laid as if dead for at least three days and still felt a sharp pain in his side, he queried how he had lived and felt some magic had played a part, Artu sensed he had an unknown ally somewhere within the woods. For centuries he and his herd had roamed freely and at times would take the fountain to other times, they however considered Brown Folly Woods their home, never before though had they seen so much of man and the attack was scary and a daunting threat. Adelleta bravely searched by his side, he hardly dare speak to her knowing she barely coped with Arrietta gone, he had to admit to himself that his beloved Arrietta's chances were very slim, he feared the worse, if she had been taken, he also knew that the captor would be back. Hartol his good friend had tracked the man and horse as far as he could, his trail had gone cold at the river, Hartol saw the boats and wondered if this had been the attackers escape. He had no idea how to find Arrietta it was hopeless, to follow the river himself was futile, the rider could have taken either direction, he could only stay and hope for her return. With heavy hearts the herd continued to search and would never give up just in case she lay alone, they had all the forest creatures searching though and surely by now something would have been found. Artu went in search of Hartol to see if he had any more news, he found him in the Dell, they talked of the horror of the attack and dear Arrietta's fate. The herd of Fauns and Hartol all thought of the hermit, they had all seen the strange one who lived alone deep in the woods, Hartol knew she was of no harm to them, he had seen her help animals and perform nothing less than magic, he suggested that they visited the strange and allusive one in hope of more information, so that day they followed the deep wooded path that they rarely trod, Hartol and Artu took great care, the path was rocky with roots arching from the earth, a steep rocky bank rose up high on one side and a deep ravine to the other, it was little wonder that not many would take the dark path, eventually the ground became easier and hidden by thicket they saw a tiny wooden shack made from sticks, fallen trees and moss. The stranger stood waiting as though she knew of their arrival she spoke first and greeted them kindly, without question she told them everything she had seen on the day of the attack, she herself had tried to save Arrietta in vain, the war horse and man were fast and strong, a black rook then swept to the ground cawing, as if to cue the strange woman to say more; she chuckled and fed the black rook a scrap, then explained the rook was her pet and a good spy called Eudes, the strange lady continued her tale explaining that Eudes had carried on following the war man in black, with the rearing black horse, he boarded a huge boat with elaborate decoration, the boat went east on the river and was rowed by a small strong army, she then chuckled again, looking them both in the eye, she told them there was some hope, for she played a little trick on the war man, whilst he dallied in the woods, she had meddled with his neatly packaged food parcel and swapped his parsley for hemlock, he would only last a few more days, shocked by her statement little was said, Artu however now felt there was some hope. They know knew that Arrietta had definitely been taken, Artu would not give up hope, something in his heart felt sure she was a live, he could only stay and wait in the woods, with heads hung still low with worry Hartol and Artu walked back towards the Dell, they talked of the strange woman who called herself Sally, Artu knew another name for her, a Wicca, he had pondered this and thought on their side

she could be useful and she showed genuine care for the loss of Arrietta, so they agreed with caution they would share their worlds
in hope Sally in the woods could help them with their human
problem. Hartol felt sure she was somehow a link he remembered
something about her in the past and as the evening drew on, he recalled a day many moons ago when the Star peoGazers had travelled through the waterfall leaving the book of Moirai, one was left
behind and he recollected the face, Sally was the child who cried
when Hehet left to join the Gods, she was the one that ran and
howled through the woods for weeks, all this time she had hidden
well, past mischiefs and strange happenings on the track in the
woods suddenly all made sense, hartol would now keep her in his
sights and Sally in the woods as a friend that he would respect and
now need by his side.

CAMBRIDGE TO OXFORD FOR A BIBBLE

1376

Hugh followed the river track out of Cambridge the boats lit the way with their candles flickering by the path, the children and adults who worked at the mill walked a long the track, with their heads down carrying meagre meals in cloth, with jugs of what ever they could find to drink, for the hard day a head toiling in the dusty deadly mill, some children as young as six dragged their sore feet, scared of the day ahead, they would be shouted at and worse and would be lucky to come home with no injury, if they came home at all. Hugh often struggled with his conscience as he sat with a full plate and comfortable room as others had nothing and worked so hard, he was blessed with his position in the monastery, Hugh also though wondered what his life would have been like had he not been adopted by the brothers of the monastery. To lift his thoughts a little light started to lift the skies as the dawn began and the birds chanted their ensemble of the day, his cart rattled along the bumpy track, Struddle briskly trotted eager and happy to be free of the confinement of the stable, with a belly full of oats she had plentiful energy. Hugh did not dare check on Arrietta concealed in sacks, they would soon be in the woods, he planned once they were well hidden by the wooded paths, he would let her run along by the cart, a little exercise was needed for her leg that seemed to have heeled so well, she had to build her strength back up some how, Hugh could not believe how smoothly his departure had gone and that he managed to keep Arrietta a complete secret, she had since told him more of her capture and described her captor, Hugh realised she had been fortuitous and had had a very lucky escape, he now knew it was the Black Prince who had taken her and had he have lived, Hugh had dreaded to thing what would have happened to Arrietta and her herd, Prince Edward the Black Prince was not known for his altruism and he felt sure poor Arrietta would have suffered an awful fate, he shuddered to think what could have been and felt so glad she lay safely in his cart, with Struddle happily trotting in front. As the world started to wake Struddle entered the forge, water splashed up and she quick-end her pace to get through the chilly water, Hugh heard Arrietta give a little squeal, as the cart tipped to one side he reassured her and Struddle all was well, quickly they were out of the water and into the woods, Hugh guided Struddle down onto the left track were a stone marked the way to Oxford, he felt a rush of excitement to think he would soon be staying in Dunstable Priory and then on to Oxford to stay in one of the wonderful quads, he had arranged to meet a dear old friend who was once at Cambridge, Edwin was a stone mason and unlike some of his work companions, he was a quiet and an educated type who enjoyed Hughs company, they had spent many a night sharing knowledge over a biddle, he looked forward to a drink of mead and good chat with his friend, Hugh had decided though he would tell know one of Arrietta he had to protect her no man or woman could be trusted. The weather was kind to Hugh on his journey and the sun rays found the depths of the woodland sparkling on the moss and leaves, Hugh pulled over the cart and spoke to Arrietta, nervously with help she was lifted from the cart and was soon on her four delicate legs, gangly at first she struggled to stand then slowly Arrietta found her strength and with glee began to walk with the forest floor beneath her, she was free, Hugh told her to go steady and stay close by, Arrietta did as she was told with a little prance, she managed many miles and walked besides Struddle who nuzzled her when they stopped, the woodland had started to thin and Hugh felt nervous, for some reason his instinct was to get Arrietta hidden and just as he had placed the sack over her in the cart a thundering noise approached, he quickly pulled Struddle of the track and as far as he could into the wood, holding Struddles head and calming her, he waited as the noise grew louder, Hugh shuddered as he saw an army at pace thundering past on their horses all in armour with terrifying weapons, some battle was a foot somewhere near, brother Hugh had a problem now he needed to get off the track and find away through the wood, more would certainly come, he could not risk being searched and the knights on horse back would have no care for a monk, they would however be interested in Arrietta. Hugh got the map out that brother Cuthbert had given him, now very thankful he had it, as it showed paths that were old and untrodden, they had just passed a folly and the tiny Church of St Faiths in the wooded hamlet named Hegestanestone, so Hugh knew where he was, if he crossed the main track he could follow an old path that would be slower but far safer, quickly Hugh urged Struddle on and soon they were deep in the wood again and although more bushy and narrow the path was fine for the small cart with a light load and Struddle's stocky small frame, Hugh heard another rumble above as horses, knights and weapons galloped past, relieved he urged Struddle on and agreed with Arrietta she should now stay hidden, the small party rested and ate and drank by a small brook all a little nervous after the close encounter, Hugh studied the map again and found a path that would save them a good hour, brother Cuthbert's map was certainly a God send it was almost magical to Hugh and had served them well. Several hours later tired and muddy, Hugh, Struddle and the cart trundled into the vast cobbled entrance of Dunstable Priory, the huge wooden gates were opened, surrounded by the facade of a castle, the court yard was huge, Hugh was quickly greeted by a stable serf, who he politely dismissed from taking Struddle explaining she would only bite and kick him, Hugh instead asked to be shown a stable or stall far from any other, the terrified serf ran ahead, pointing to where the vicious pony could go, he then scampered of never to be seen again by Hugh on his short visit, Hugh sorted out Struddle and hid Arrietta in his stall, he was unhappy with the situation, anyone could easily peek over the stalls low wooden dividers and the biting wind blew straight through, Hugh thought what to do, not only was it unsafe it was also chilly and damp, he worried poor Arrietta would freeze, Hugh asked Arrietta to stay well hidden under the sack he put in the stall, explaining he would be back soon,Hugh then walked as quickly as possible over to the enormous priory and round entrance, he was greeted to his surprise, with such cheer and hospitality, many shook his hand and asked after Abbot James, he was clearly a very well respected and thought of brother by the monks at Dunstable Priory, Hugh was seated and fed well he was then shown to his chamber, Hugh explained he would pray alone due to his exhaustion and need to leave incredibly early, with no question he was left alone, his small chamber was perfect it was in a far corner on the ground floor facing outwards the square and not into the cloisters, Hugh carefully climbed through his window into the now dark night, he found his way back to the stalls and moved both Struddle and Arrietta, he had found a row of larger stables that had gigantic shire horses in, Hugh quickly filled an empty stall with hay and water and taking more sacks and straw Hugh settled them all in the stable, they now had no chilling wind and warmth from their giant companions, the huge horses made the stables cosy and safe, the three spent the night quite comfortably in a deep sleep and with the first tweet of a bird the following day, They were up and out of the stable and monastery gates, long before the bustle of the Priory woke, with it's friendly and wonderful greetings, brother James had mentioned their great hospitality and Hugh would liked to have tasted their breakfast, as he thought of the delicious meal he had had for his supper, instead though he munched on apples and pony oats, faithfully Struddle trotted on with her oat filled nose bag, bobbing along, they had a long journey a head across country with no river to guide and only endless woodlands, Struddle was sound though and covered the soft paths with no trouble, the long tree lined journey seemed to pass quickly with no events. Hugh and his small company broke from the forests and arrived into pretty meadows they crossed the River Cherwell and

followed the path across Christ Church Meadow and were suddenly in the glorious city of scholars, a bustle of students, monks
and trades people was wonderful, music played and the fires
burnt, smells of food and spices filled the air, brother Hugh felt as
though he was a great explorer, with pride he arrived at his Oxford
lodgings, he insisted on sorting his own horse saying she was
nasty again to strangers, sweet Struddle of course would never
hurt a fly, this allowed Hugh to hide Arrietta in her stable again,
warm and safe while Hugh had to leave them, no one would enter
afraid of the treacherous pony, a cross was chalked on the door a
sign to others not to enter. Struddle and Arrietta drank and ate
and Hugh managed to sneak in extra food for them, he promised
to check on them later and with a skip in his step and sense of freedom he went to meet Edwin for a biddle in the Bear Inn. Meeting
his friend for a cup of a mead was a true treat for a monk in such a
place, they found a quieter corner and Hugh tried to ignore the
garish laughter and comments, soon the crowd ignored him and
carried on with the normal nights banter, giving Hugh and his
friend Edwin time to chat and catch up, Edwin had good news he
was to start some masonry work at the Abbey in Bath, so was
thrilled Hugh would be there with his exciting botanical project,
Hugh confessed to caring little for the Abbot, he however knew it
was a good opportunity for him, at that point, He wished he could
tell Edwin of Arrietta, although he kept his own word afraid of the
consequences, before the evening grew to late and the crowd to
raucous, Edwin and Hugh wished each other safe travels and with
Gods speed that they should soon be together in Bath. Hugh hurried off, to check on the stable and was happy to find them undisturbed, still afraid though he gathered his belongings and small
parcel for the abbot, leaving his meek room he joined Struddle and
Arrietta, preferring their company instead of being alone in a cold
stone room. He slept well full of mead and when the cockerel
crowed and the bells rang, Hugh was already clean and dressed,
with Struddle and Arrietta well feed and watered, Hugh took his
leave to look at the beauty of the priory St Frideswide, he decided
to stay as anonymous as possible, keen to continue his journey

alone, so with his head down and hood firmly on he held his prayer book and beads, in his prayer book old brother Gerald had written down some parts of interest, he would love for Hugh to see, Hugh was humbled to see the shrine, carved beautifully with vines, doves and faces, he gazed at its beauty, he then looked at the arches and great door with spectacular carvings and gargoyles that stared down as if watching his every move, he marvelled at Christ Church and many other places, he spent a little while in wonder at the beautiful Osney Abbey, transfixed by its water wheel that ran the mill on Osney Island, the spell was broken by the loudest bell he had ever heard named Great Tom it bellowed out a cross the city, Hugh took this as a good sign to move on, happy with his morning Hugh bought some lunch from a street trader and sat by the river and contemplated his journey home, he knew the track would be busy this though was safer for him, as it was a journey known for outlaws with so much produce and spice being transported to London. A little nervous Hugh went back to the stable and packed up, the stables were quiet as everyone took lunch and afternoon prayer, his absence would never be noted and as quietly as he arrived he left, Hugh and his small cart were soon following the busy river track down to Dorchester-on-Thames and the Abbey, where he would meet brother Hector to collect his delivery of exotic plants, herbs and seeds. The morning was kind to them with a gentle spring breeze and generous sprinkling of sunshine, Arrietta had agreed to stay hidden, although when quiet Hugh would give her word and she would stare out at the passing scenery and sniff the glorious morning air, Hugh pointed things out to her and she made little squeals of delight at the ducklings paddling along the river and swifts diving through the blue skies, in a wooded area she saw a young fawn much like her, without the human part, she whinnied in hope it would hear, it took flight though, flicking its white tale as it jumped into the depths of foliage. The journey was a pretty one and most seemed to travel the other way, Hugh felt at ease he was however glad later that day to see the stone marked for Dorchester on the Thames, he saw the huge structure and church tower, masons chiseled, heaved and built the Abbey that grew up to the heavens, set in a tiny hamlet of cottages, there were still the remains of the roman fort, that was once a strong hold due to its perfect location on the river, now a deeply religious settlement Hugh was eager to take look around, later he found the Inn where he had lodgings at the stable and tended to Struddle, pleased with her longevity and eagerness, he spoilt her with apples and carrots, followed by an early oat and linseed super with fresh spring water, he rubbed her down carefully and gave her ample hay, the stables were better stocked than most homes and Struddle stood amongst some fine steeds, he also settled Arrietta who grew impatient knowing she grew closer to home, Hugh could sense her need to run and be free, sweet and prudent though she listened to his reason and her fear of being captured again kept her well hidden in the stall. Hugh went into the Inn and enjoyed a large tanker of mead, this though tasted different from the heavy Oxford brew, in the Bear Inn, this had a lightness he liked, Hugh had only waited for a little while, when brother Hector walked in, Hugh had never met Hector before, his description though was accurate in every detail, his long white beard and vivid green eyes struck you first, then his warming smile and large welcoming stance, he looked godly as though he came from another time and when he spoke his words sounded magical and poetical. Hugh immediately liked him greatly and was eager to learn from this scholar of Botany and so much more, Hugh would have loved to have spent so much more time with him and ask so many questions, they both gladly ate meat pie and drank, while Hugh listened to his wonderful stories of travel and other lands, to Hugh they sounded unworldly and mystifying. Hector and Hugh eventually a little merry went outside and set forth to transfer the herbs, seeds, plugs and plants into his cart, Hector insisted on placing them himself in order and with detailed instruction, Hugh could only watch as the master delicately placed each with such care, upon each muslin parcel there was a small scroll with its name and instruction, eventually he was packed, brother Hector chatted for a while about the soil and other matters of the earth, he then said he should be off and that he would see Hugh hopefully soon, they bid each other a found fare well, Hector then vanished on the small narrow lane, Hugh rubbed his eyes, he felt he had just met a supreme being, an avatar from a different time. Exhausted he joined his four legged friends and slept like never before. The next morning Hugh set out, he crossed over a beautiful low lying meadow full of flowers that lead onto the river path that curved towards the West country, the pretty journey lead him down through acres of ancient woods far away from the Thames, he saw very few travellers, still he kept Arrietta under wraps, he knew they grew closer with every step to her home and as if Hugh had sensed her thoughts, he knew that they had arrived. Arrietta gingerly got down from the cart and what happened next Hugh would never forget for his whole life, almost instantly they were surrounded, Hugh stood in wonder at the strange mythological creatures, he did not think once about his own safety, instead he greeted them as though he had known them all his life, Arrietta stood close to his side, he was her protector and saviour, her herd needed to know he was the reason she lived, Artu cautiously walked towards the stranger, seeing Arrietta's trust in him, he thanked him many times and insisted he was welcome to grace the ancient woodlands when ever he wished and then with nuzzles and tears, Arrietta was gone, Hugh felt a little empty in one way, yet relieved in another, he hoped one day he would meet her again some how, he was unsure how he would ever find her in the vast woodlands, something told him though they would find him first. Hugh mounted back on to his cart, Struddle seemed unfazed by the experience as though it was all quite normal and they started their descent through the woods, Hugh glimpsed several times another herd of horses and felt it must be his vivid imagination that they two were half human. The huge white stag though he saw clearly, as it watched him with curiosity and it was not until Hugh had left the deep wooded paths, that he knew he was out of the realms of the magical ancient woodlands, he had heard folk tales and ghost stories, now he knew they were not tales but truths, again a secret he would keep close. Hugh stopped to check his load was secure, confused he moved a sizeable book wrapped well in muslin, he had not seen Hector put in the cart, other parcels he had collected for the Abbot at Bath were small, so presuming it was planting instructions, he carried on his way, Hugh felt a little empty, he missed Arrietta and her sweet ways, something else though joined him, he felt a presence he could not explain, his mind could not forget Hector and his god like figure, Hugh felt something beyond even his imagination had started and he began to feel that he was involved in something much grander than his simple garden and herbs, he recalled Hectors stories of lands before and the Gods, he talked then briefly of a powerful book that could change the path of life, Hugh hastened on suddenly afraid, did he carry that very book, should a guard search him by misfortune he would surely hang.

LACEY & BILLY, ARRIETTA & HUGH 1386

Lacey and Billy had lived happily in the woods, since escaping the castle, at times they were hungry and cold and spent their time hidden like fugitive's, they found the wood amazing and had discovered the Dell and mythical creatures, their lives were an adventure with constant surprises, both grew close to the white stag Hartol and thought him more human than deer, when they met Artu and his herd they were even more entranced and Lacey grew a special friendship with Arrietta and by chance she would again meet brother Hugh and hear the wonderful story of Arrietta's rescue, it was wonderful for Lacey to see brother Hugh again and he promised to keep their secret, although in truth he was saddened they had run away, Hugh felt Lacey could have made a ladies maid to royalty in time, she was bright enough he thought and special, he had seen a good future for her and now she was running wild in the woods. At first he disliked the stable boy Billy and blamed him for Lacey's demise, Hugh found though in time he was as bright as a button and witty too, he could charm the wool of a sheep on a winters day. Hugh saw they were content to be together and that they never thought about their future or what it would bring, he could see they never wished to give up their freedom, Hugh knew though deep down as they grew older their life would be harder and they were bound to be captured in time. For as long as he could he would visit them and help in any small ways he could. Lacey and Billy would be taught to read and write a skill that was only for scholars, brother Hugh would call regularly to see his dear Faun friend Arrietta, with Lacey and Billy, an unlikely combination of companions, they would share many happy days in the spring and summer months, wandering in the glades and ferns of Brown Folly Woods. It was then that Hugh would reflect on all the problems of the land and prayed someone would stop such destruction of woodland and nature, he would often look at Billy and say some young man should bid parliament for no felling unless deemed necessary and to stop clearing for senseless deer parks, merely for hunting, they had open land enough for sheep, he worried not knowing where it would all end. Hugh had spoken often with Arrietta about his fears for the future of the precious Dell and magical spring waters, he understood its significance to the woodlands, Hugh simplified this amazing and mind blowing phenomenon as being the heart of the worlds ancient woodlands, if it was to die so would the rest of the old enchanted woodland in the world. Mythical creatures and all would be gone forever, this a sadness he could share with no one other than them. Hugh would spend his time between the monastery and woods, his fortune was his study of Botany and the Dell became a constant source of new wonders and his gardens in the hot spring was becoming famous in its own right, brother Hugh was considered a genius a creator in his field, an explorer and naturalist, with such a passion to drive him and with his ancient knowledge from the Fauns and Hartol he had endless theories, Hugh was careful though not too upset or create any suspicion that he did not follow the good lords word and the beliefs of his brothers and the religious tyranny of his King. He now held and often read the book not of botany but of something colossal, something he did not yet fully understand, in time though he began to envisage the essence and supremacy of the mystifyingly book brother Hector had slipped in his cart on that fine spring day.

TOM & SARAH ANOTHER STRANGE MEET 1721

Things had been busy at home for Sarah, her Ma and Pa had lots of work at the Manor and she was often left with Bobby, he grew and now crawled, so Sarah was often dragging him out of the coal bucket or grabbing him before he descended at speed down the narrow stairs, she never protested and looked after him as best as she could, she had seen little of Tom lately and had heard that things at his home were not good, his Ma was very poorly and was bed ridden so she knew dear Tom would be at her side. It was a beautiful warm day and Sarah knew she would be left until late, so she strapped Bobby into the cart with some rope and set off a cross the fields, Sarah needed to see Tom and although she was unsure if it was the best thing to do, she convinced herself that it was the only thing to do, she had to discus the Dell and more, she longed to go back, although understood that Tom may not be able to yet, they had both promised they would never go alone. Sarah arrived at Tom's cottage the windows were all open and she could see Tom at the front of the house, Sarah cautiously approached and tried to make it look as though she was just passing by, Tom saw her and waved, relived she went up to him dragging the heavy cart as Bobby made strange growling noises, he had decided to do dog impressions for some reason. Sarah got closer to Tom and could see he had been crying she ignored this and brightly greeted him, Tom asked if she had time to walk, Sarah explained she had all day, so as normal with little words off they went, as Sarah turned to check on Bobby she noticed the Doctor was in the cottage door way, Sarah knew this was bad news the Doctor only came for a serious reason, she ignored her sighting and with her tongue held for little while, she followed Tom who walked unusually fast, Sarah struggled to keep, Tom looked back and apologetically came back and helped her pull the cart, Bobby continued to growl, Tom looked quizzically at Sarah and they both laughed together, Bobby continued to growl as he heard their laughter. Without thinking they both walked in a daze towards the woods and were drawn along the path that led to the Dell. Tom was deep in thought and Sarah respected his silence, she felt he wanted some answers and as they arrived into the magical world of the crystal pool and Dell, they saw more mystical wonders, stood with the white stag, was a deer half man, half stag and with him a herd of the same mythical creatures that rested and grazed on the soft mossy grass, the males had antlers and the females long manes,Tom and Sarah could not help but gasp, their presence was not ignored and the white stag Hartol settled the herd explaining that they were safe humans. The large mythical stag introduced himself as Artu and gave the names of his family Adelleta and Arrietta, Arrietta came over to them and introduced herself she was tall and graceful her hair like a flowing main shone around her lovely face and deer like eyes, she said not to be afraid they were gentle creatures, she said they had been around for hundreds of years and today they met in fear of humans who took the forest for their land, they all sort to find away to protect the ancient woodlands. Sarah gently stroked Arrietta's soft fur and asked her what ever could they do, Arrietta smiled gently at her and told her they had a plan, it was a complicated one though and needed careful arrangements to take place. Arrietta went to sit back with her herd the mythical Fauns and Hartol all settled, as Lacey and Billy arrived in there ghostly forms, Sarah went to great her friends as she looked for Mary who was no where to be seen, Lacey held out her hands in a comforting gesture and said it was good she was gone, she was at peace. Without thinking through her tears Sarah asked out loud why they were they ghosts and why were they here and how had they died, she knew Mary had died of the fever, Sarah wanted to know why Mary had been a ghost with them and she looked at Tom and saw his smile, she knew he thought the same thoughts as her. Lacey asked them to sit so Tom and Sarah sat on the soft mossy floor near the crystal pool, they looked at the strange deer and admired their beauty, they looked at the white stag and everything around them and then they just listened to Lacey's sweet voice as she almost sang her story.

A PLAQUE ORA WITCH

Lacey said they stayed in the forest the year that they escaped from the castle and the following year bought a hard cold winter, an out break of the curse the black death was back, so they kept far from people and Hartol and the Faun herd terrified they could give them the plague, they lived off the woods and travelled deeper afraid of meeting some one passing through, that was when they met Sally and she was not happy to have them in her domain, so sent them skipping, Lacey said Sally was a witch and she had no care for people, she only liked animals, she said the black death was a punishment a curse to kill of people for all the wrongs they did. Lacey said they were terrified of her and ran, they heard her cackling as they left and often they would see her flying through the trees in her white robes, they hid well from her and never went near her hovel again. Billy though thought she had put a curse on them, for he felt ill so soon after meeting her, Lacey tried every-thing to keep him alive, the cold crept in though and with no sup-plies and little food and a fever, poor Billy had no hope, Lacey wrapped him in the sheep wool he had found a week before on an abandoned cart and set off to find brother Hugh, she waited for him on the track stepping out in hope at each horse or cart that travelled by, her thin white frock was no help in the biting winds so exhausted and defeated she gave up and plodded back to her Billy, only to find him like an ice block , with strange black boils; the witches curse, afraid and alone Lacey said she waited and waited for her Billy to come back, she couldn't live without Billy and she drifted away one bitter night as ice set deep in the woods and waters, the earth stood frozen and still. Lacey sighed and smiled at Tom and Sarah and Hartol broke the silence he spoke in his deep gentle voice Tom and Sarah were shocked at first they had never heard him speak before, they expected the Fauns to being half human. Hartol began his tale of events telling them in the summer a monk called brother Hugh had hatched a plan with both Billy, Lacey and Arrietta it was risky and almost impossible, he planned with the Fauns help to send Lacey and Billy back in time with their new skills and knowledge, Billy and Lacey were going to save the ancient woods with Hugh and the beguiling book he possessed, he knew he could convince others, Hugh had felt confident it was possible with the King of that time. Hartol looked sad and said we never thought they would die that winter, the plan was lost, brother Hugh tried all his life to save the ancient woods, he never found any who could replace Lacey and Billy to carry out the proposal. Had Lacey and Billy though been able to carry out the plan they would have saved more and changed the path of man. Hartol was sad they had lost the Centaurs from the woodland forever and they could not return. Tom was not sure what he meant by any of this and asked again why some came back as ghosts. Hartol replied, Lacey and Billy could never leave, they still felt bound to carry out brother Hugh's wishes, as ghosts, though they could never go back through the waterfall to another time, they stay like other ghosts because they can't let go, some linger a little and others never go, they can only do so when they are at peace and ready to leave their loved ones behind or their unfinished quests. Tom was suddenly overwhelmed with devastation, the words rang through his head, some spirits of the dead stayed when they wanted to see someone again and couldn't let go. Tom turned and ran with tears streaming down his face, his Ma had died only that morning and she didn't come to see him, she didn't want to say one last goodbye, she didn't mind letting go. Tom did not no where he ran the woods were darker and he had never been this far before, he bolted down a treacherous path, Tom stumbled, tripping over a root and fell, he kept falling and falling he crashed to the bottom and lay still and lifeless in the ravine inches from the rivers icy waters that crashed with no mercy on the cold hard rocks.

THE RETURN OF THE PLAQUE 1387

The bubonic plaque had swept through Asia and arrived in Europe in 1347, twelve ships sailed and docked at Messina on board those poor ships, was a horror never seen before, the ships were filled with the piteous dead or dying, the death ships were ordered out of the port, sadly the plaque had arrived though and nothing could stop it from reaching every shore and shire, its effects were devastating and loss of life was huge, traumatic and cruel, for years it continued to rear up with a cruel vengeance from nowhere. Fifty-two years later it would pay a another unwelcome visit to the sleepy valleys of the South, the wool trade had recovered from the death of so many sheep and people from the plagues first visit, so when it was discovered again, panic spread like wild fire and people this time learnt to isolate and abandon the dying. The plague was first discovered on a track five furlongs from Farliegh Castle, a young merchant delivering wool would be found slumped and dead on his cart, with the telltale black boils of the plague, he was burnt with no empathy and his death cart lay foolishly abandoned full of wool sacks. Many would take from the wool sacks on the cart, including a young boy from the woods and sadly again the plaque spread with no regard to who it reached. Farliegh Castle herd the news of the out break and locked its huge gates a natural fortress with its cliff like edges to three sides, no one would enter or leave any one who showed even the smallest symptom would be banished to the outer walls of the moat, food and water would be left on the steps, a bell was rung and the fetcher would disappear, the doomed who were outcast would perish of the cold before the dastardly plaque would finished them off, the castle still took deliveries of supplies and many would die within those strong castle walls and the surrounding villages and towns, the Hungerford family themselves lost a daughter and her children, a loss their father would never accept. The year was savage and sombre for all, loved ones were lost and times were hard, produce dwindled as crops had not been tendered and animals died from no care. The desperate folk carried on as best as they could to harvest for the winter, they battened down the hatches for one of the cruelest, coldest and hardest season ever sent to the gentle valleys and woodlands, the landscape glistened in a frosting deeper than any had known before, frozen and abandoned they waited in prayer for some miracle, no saviour arrived and the freeze held for many more long months only to be broken by a ruthless and endless rain with little hope for any end.

THE ORIGIN OF SALLY 800 AD

Sally was born as Sarah in the year 800 the daughter of King Eardwulf of Northumbria, like her mother she was gifted the glossiest black hair and beautiful complexion, adored she was dressed in the finest robes the King and Queen Eardwulf could find, the youngest and only daughter she was a joy to their hearts. Sarah was only six years old, when her Father was forced into exile, although he would one day return as ruler, a cruel political game was played by other noble men, causing the murders of her elder brothers and the cruel kidnap of Sarah, she was taken and never seen again, presumed dead the King and Queen grieved, with no reason to think she was alive they never looked. Sarah's kidnap was arranged by an enemy of the King with ease and she was quickly given to a caravan of people called the Star Gazers, no one would question them as she looked just like travellers who looked to the stars, who were glad of copper coins and a strong girl, they happily took her away with no clue of her royalty and grieving monarchy left far behind. Sarah would soon be renamed Sally, she was no longer a Princess waited on and tended to, she would now be treated like any other, Sally though was lucky and would be taken in by Meriiti, who was kind to her and needed an assistant, Sally would learn everything from Meriiti, she would learn what Mer called Hecka, with a cackle and a little magic. For Sally this became a surprisingly happy time, she loved Meriiti and enjoyed being with all the lively and colourfully dressed people, each day would consist of travelling and each night would be around camp fires, Sally would try delicious spices and herbs, Meriiti would teach her how to cook and weave, she would also teach Sally the art of potions and painting with strange symbols. Meriiti was well respected within the group and they had no trouble from others with respect for their healing powers, the nomadic Star Gazers stayed together and ignored hostility, sometimes they would have no option other than to fight to defend themselves, most would leave them alone though because they were afraid of their ways and looks. The Star Gazers travelled south they sought the hot springs they had heard off in the marshes, they had also heard of a magical place, a sacred sight that they wished to pay homage to a place where they could please the Gods and travel to the other times. Meriiti had been searching the skies and looking at old scriptures to find the sacred Dell deep in ancient woodland, they knew they grew closer after centuries of searching, they camped that night in the deep woods and made make shift huts with fallen branches, creating a small settlement, they were visited the next day early in the dawn by a strange herd of Fauns and a white stag, the Star Gazers showed the enquiring creatures many rituals and spiritual dances with prayers and song, trusting and convinced of their pureness they were allowed to follow and go to the Dell and see the crystal pool and waterfall, In wonder the Star Gazers cried tears of joy the legends were true, for so long they had search and one by one they would enter the pool and simply disappear, obediently they stood in a peaceful line humming and chanting until it was their own turn, when it came to Meriiti she turned to Sally who stood shaking with fear, unsure quite what was happening to everyone, Meriiti tried to explain it was a gateway to another time, the time of the Gods, she stroked Sally's hair gently and with tears said she could not come, Meriiti whispered to take the waters of the crystal pool and always remember her magical powers that she had taught her, she passed Sally her precious and ancient book to hide in the waterfall and with tears rolling down her cheeks, she left Sally standing alone with the Faun's and stag, each watched the Star Gazer's return to their Gods, the last two a strange girl and boy hesitantly looked back and smiled at Sally, then hand in hand they went like the others. Sally sobbed and when there was no hope of her peoples return, she threw the book in rage and she ran and ran, when she came to a track, she stopped dead and screamed, her scream echoed through the ancient wood, the birds were silent and the animals did not rustle, they sensed a presence never known before, for Sally had arrived into the woods and there she would stay, looking and hoping one day her people would return to find her and then once again she could look into the soft brown eyes of Meriiti who she loved with all her heart. Hartol the white stag saved the book and hid it carefully in the rocks of the fountain of time.

SALLY THE WATCHER

Sally saw many things in the woods, she had seen battles and men die, she saw people on the run and she saw lost people wander forever, Sally was their the night they had hunted the herd of Fauns and she herself panicked and tried to help as best as she could, she loved the Fauns they made her smile, the evil knight in black was cruel, she could smell it on his aroma and he fought Artu near to death, Sally had summoned all her powers the Black Prince though gave a deadly blow and took the young Faun little Arrietta, distraught Sally followed, she prayed Arrietta would be well knowing her captor had not long to live, with her meddling, she hastened her spy Eudes the Rook to follow. Sally raced back to Artu and mixed balms and pastes, she poured heeling herbs in his mouth and sat vigil with him. Eventually he stirred and Sally was gone. The day Arrietta came back was one of joy and Arrietta knew somehow that Sally had helped and she made her a friend like brother Hugh, Sally loved Arrietta and her softy brown eyes and suddenly she didn't feel quite so lonely. Sally had also seen other woodland guests, she watched the girl and the boy, who had escaped from the castle. Sally had spied on them in the woods since their arrival, she wanted to be friends, she liked their quiet ways and sweet friendship that she envied, Sally felt sad, after all those years she was still alone and often thought of Meriiti, she had she would come back for her one day, with each year that was scratched away, she began to realise Meriiti would not return. Sally loved all the creatures of the woods she considered them her friends, Sally tutted to herself as she thought of brother Hugh, he was found of the girl and boy and he became a good friend to her, a friendship of herbs they would say, how he had grieved the girl and boy that died, as though they were his own flesh and blood, Sally told him she knew they would both die, she had sent them away from her hut, she said they carried the black death and there was nothing she could do for them, she chanted for them and tried to scare the evil spirits away, nothing would work and sadly she felt their little lives go and in place their spirits that stayed, Sally knew they were scared of her even as little ghosts, she still watched them and found them pleasing, even as spirits they were happy and free. Brother Hugh though was so sad and so frustrated, Sally tried to help him with his grief, just as she could not save them though, she could not help him, other than to show him new plants and share her knowledge, she had learnt in hope it would find its way into books of learning for others to see, she knew her knowledge was precious and not from this place or time and to not to share would have made everything seem worthless. Sally walked and flew through the woods, she liked to scare people on the track and just like little Lacey's ghost, she would make people jump and fall of their horses or send their cart off course, it helped to keep the humans away, rumours spread and the woods were feared, with their strange goings on. Sally watched everything and sensed trouble, she saw him come that dark afternoon, clumsily running and crying he crashed with no care into trunks and bushes, he seemed blind by his anger and he ran faster and faster, then she heard his cry as he fell down into the deep dark ravine and there he lay, still as a stick and pale as snow, Sally flew down, she carefully glided close and smelt his tiny breath near death, with all her might she bundled him up and flew him back to her hovel. Sally heard their calls, afraid she would be blamed though she hid him well and just like Artu, she covered him in balms and pastes and gave him herb tonics in droplets, Sally covered him in blankets and lit the fire, she sat by his side chanting her prayers, the night would come and go for Tom with little change, then Sally took him back to his own bed, he would wake with no clue of what lay behind and what now lay ahead for him.

SARAH'S LIE 1721

Sarah had raced after Tom but lost him, the others had tried to help they searched and called with no sight or sound and as the darkness crept to every path, Artu beckoned Sarah to go home, worried for her safety they took her to the edge of the wood, Sarah promised she would not say a word they could not risk a search party in the woods and she was certain Tom would be found tonight under the rising moon, Artu, Adelleta and Arrietta promised they would search all night, trusting them Sarah took Bobby back in his rackety cart, she fixed his mashed potato supper, not able to eat herself, Sarah sat by the embers of the range, her parents were late and their sudden home coming made her jump, her Pa hugged her and told her the news that Tom's Ma had died and Tom had run away, Sarah cried and cried and breathed not one word, her Ma asked if she had seen him at all that day, thinking of the doctor, who would have glimpsed her and Bobby's cart, with her fingers crossed behind her back Sarah told her lie, she said that she had chatted briefly with Tom whilst passing, he had mentioned Bath and walked in that direction. Sarah's Pa hugged her and headed for the door saying he was going to find Tom's Pa, they would go to Bath to look for him. Sarah prayed for forgiveness as she lay awake, the moon flickered through window, the moving branches on the tree outside cast a strange claw like shadows on her wall, Sarah felt scared and was worried beyond belief, she thought of Tom out in the woods all alone, she prayed they had found him, Sarah knew her lie was bad, if Tom was never found she would always know he was in the woods somewhere alone, she tossed and turned and wrestled with her lie, her Pa had not come back and she knew the morning was waiting to come, Sarah would not sleep she stroked little Bobby and prayed and prayed, strangely deep down Sarah knew Tom was going to be fine, she could never explain it but those spirits and creatures and others in the woods would help Tom, she convinced herself and finally found a little sleep and was shortly woken to the noise of her Pa and Tom's Pa they sounded drunk and very loud, Sarah afraid listened to their jeering and then Tom's Pa's crying, she heard her Ma go down to see what was going on and she heard the men say they both celebrated and morned, missing Tom had been found tucked up in his bed sleeping like a baby, while his poor Ma slept forever in the parlour, relieved and sad Sarah wondered how an earth he had found his way back in the darkness, maybe the moon had shown him the way or Hartol or something else. Sarah tossed and turned until the dawn finally lit the morning skies in full, she waited for Bobby to wake, then took him downstairs for his milk and pottage, her Ma and Pa had already left, her Ma had to be up at the hall to get everything ready for the breakfasts and her Pa would have walked Ma to work, where he would have his breakfast before starting the day in the gardens. Sarah didn't mind being alone with Bobby, since Mary had gone it seemed easier not to have to look at her Ma's face and see her hurt, she knew she was never going to get over loosing Mary, Sarah thought perhaps she was her favourite, she certainly cared nothing for little Bobby and was only kind to Sarah because she was of use to her, Sarah didn't feel cross towards her though, she strangely for someone so young understood. After breakfast she took Bobby out, there was a strange mist hanging over the valley with no view could be seen, Sarah took the short cut through the wood and across the field arriving at Tom's cottage, she could see smoke from the chimney, which was strange even with the mist it wasn't cold, she walked around to the back and listened, deciding Tom's Pa had already gone to work, she walked in through the back door carrying Bobby, she avoided the parlour and quietly like a little mouse walked up the stairs, Sarah found Tom's room easily in the tiny cottage and nervously opened the door, Tom lay white as a sheet in bed his fire flickered giving of a strange yet

pleasant herbal smell and sat by him rubbing ointment on his
wrist was the strangest person Sarah had ever seen, she was
dressed all in white and had long dark curls, her face was young
yet strangely old, her eyes held the worlds woes and a twinkle that
was hard to explain, they were blue yet green with a hint of brown,
her complexion was glowing yet strangely it looked almost bronze
and then rosy and then as dark as her own brown eyes, she mumbled in words Sarah did not understand and in that small moment
of time, Sarah saw strange flashes of images of similar people dash
through her mind, the other people like this strange lady dressed
in white, she saw them in the crystal pool and she felt sad and
tears rolled down her cheeks, the trance was broken and the
strange being turned like a damsel fly and flittered around, she
eyed Sarah up and down and then let out an enormous sigh, then
she just smiled the prettiest smile Sarah had ever seen and her old
yet young face lit up like a star in the sky, she touched Sarah's hand
gently and called her my Meriiti. Sarah was very confused and felt
awfully strange, she however needed to know wether or not Tom
was ok, he looked so pale and his breath could not be seen, the
strange woman saw her concern and told her all about how she
had found him in the deep ravine and how the icy water tried to
take him, she reassured Sarah that he would be fine, he slept
deeply because she had given him a sleep potion, that would heel
his head and make him rest until he was better, Sarah with hesi-
tance asked who she was and Sally introduced herself and then
she talked about Meriiti and how Meriiti had left her long, long
ago by the crystal pool and how she always believed she would
come back, Sally rambled on about how she saw her in her eyes
and how Meriiti would have chosen the name Sarah the name of a
Princess, Sarah was shocked and flummoxed inside, she managed
though to remain calm outwardly, not wanting to upset the
strange lady, she accepted Sally's strange notion that her dear lost
friend was her somehow, Sarah then dared ask how long ago
meriiti left her, Sally tapped on the chair with her long nails, she
cackled a little and said it was along time ago, maybe nine hundred
years or more, Sarah gasped, she looked closely at Sally trying to

decide if the she was barking mad or truly was the oldest human on earth, Sarah didn't really care at that moment though all she cared about was Tom and when he would wake and if he would be the same when he did. Sally reassured her again as if she read her mind, Bobby then started to growl and to both their shock they heard some one on the stairs, Sarah panicked knowing it would be bad if Sally was found by Tom's bed, she turned to see Sally's chair was empty, she had simply vanished, then the door opened and in stepped Sarah's worst nightmare, Mother Darcey, she started straight away with her infuriating chatter, without drawing breath, she clattered on about how it was all very strange, how Tom had disappeared then lay like death tucked up in bed and where had the strange smell come from, why was the fire lit on a mild day and why was he was paler than a ghost and how his breath was far to low, Sarah of course agreed it was strange, Mother Darcey continued to jabber and jabber on, she felt Tom's head while she continued her constant mumblings, Bobby continued to give off a deep growl, every so often Mother Darcy would look at him and tut, she would then start her rant about how it was wrong for a young girl to care for the baby, he needed to learn words not dog talk, she said he looked to fat and told Sarah to stop feeding him so much, it took all Sarahs might not to draw Mother Darcey's attention to her own rather rotund physic, deciding it was not worth the battle she kept her words scrambling in her head, while begging Bobby to stop his growls. Mother Darcy started to shake Tom and Sarah knew this was wrong, she had to speak or distract the interfering pest, Sarah gave out a scream, pointing and crying to Mother Darcy that she had cockroach the size of a mouse on her back, Mother Darcy went bright red and tried desperately to flick the none existent bug of her back, while Sarah said what dirty things they were and she gasped maybe it was to do with the strange pungent smell, Mother Darcy dashed from the room and down the stairs, still wittering on, she called up to the window; whilst desperately shaking her shawl, to give him the broth and she would call some other time. Sarah so relieved she had gone sat on the bed exhausted and gently stroked

Tom's hand, she expected Sally to reappear as quickly as she had vanished, she didn't though much to Sarah's relief so she just sat there, she lifted Bobby onto the bed and he coed and cuddled Tom while he played with his favourite new stocking & button dog Sarah had made him. Sarah watched Bobby as he drifted off to sleep curled up like a puppy next to Tom, she sat still in the little bedside chair hardly daring to take her own breath, she whispered to Tom to get better and slowly her eyes closed, each time she tried to force them open like wooden shutters they closed again, until Sarah herself fell into a deep sleep, she dreamt of herself in a different land she saw a yellow earth that stretched for miles with no trees or pools or becks, she heard strange voices and she herself spoke in different words, everything was strange and different. Sarah woke slowly to see Tom sat up playing with Bobby and she heard herself mumbling those strange words, embarrassed she went bright red and pulled her shawl around her, Tom grinned and she forgot her embarrassment and praised him for being wake and seemingly well. Tom said her endless chanting in weird words had woken him up and Bobby growling, they both laughed and agreed Tom should eat the broth Mother Darcy had bought. Tom was wobbly so Sarah went to get it for him, warming it gently on the heat that remained on the stove. Once Tom had eaten all his broth and bread, Sarah told him about Sally and how she had saved him from the ravine and bought him back home, she explained as well as she could how Sally called her someone called Meriiti her ancient friend and then how the dreaded Mother Darcy had come, Tom laughed at the cockroach story, he was shocked by the Sally tale though and pressed Sarah to tell him every detail, they agreed again they had to go back to the Dell as soon as Tom was better.

SALLY'S RETREAT 1721

Sally had smelt Mother Darcy before she saw her, the unmistakeable smell of chicken broth and lavender on her clothes made Sally vanish with no trace, she had crossed paths before with her a few times over the years, Mother Darcy fancied herself as some sought of witch herself, with her useless cures and cruxes, all to often Sally had had to creep into a babies or child's room at night to fix a fever or worse, Sally sadly had been nowhere near on the night of the two Mary's, she doubted even on that occasion of sorrow she could have helped, some sadly were not curable it was as fact of life and sometimes they were a calling for something more momentous, they were special and were needed else where, just like the little Mary's who lead Sarah and Tom their way, Sally gasped to herself when she thought of Sarah so sure she was Meriiti in another form, with those soft brown unmistakeable eyes, Sally knew something was happening something pivotal, Meriiti, Sarah, the little Mary's and Tom, somehow there was a puzzle to piece together and she clicked and clucked like a chicken on her way back to her hovel in the woods. She must find Hartol and Artu they would know, for now though she had to rest the night had taken its toll, she ate a few herbs and potatoes and wrapped herself up, knowing the boy would be fine with Meriiti or Sarah, Sally drifted of to sleep and there she stayed for a couple of days, dreaming or foreseeing she was not sure, when she woke she quickly dressed and went to find Hartol, he as always was not far from the Dell patrolling and listening, he saw Sally coming and as she drank from the crystal pool, he watched her curiously and always with a little reserve, he knew she was what the humans called a witch, yet

Hartol could never really work out wether she was truly good or bad, he felt she didn't care either way and for this part he was right. Sally cared not for other humans really she saved children when she could because she liked children, adults became vengeful with agendas and complications, she did not understand or like in her humble opinion they were selfish often and did little good and more harm. Hartol stood quietly next to Sally, he dipped his long gentle face and antlers in a subservient manner, Sally looked at his huge gentle head with its deep white fur that almost glistened, his eyes were dark and gentle and he smelt of clover and daisy's, Sally told him of Tom and Sarah and how he thought she was Meriiti, she told him of her dreams or predictions, Hartol listened without interruption or doubt, he felt reassured Sally was there to help and felt certain he could now share his secret and after all this time he would put brother Hughs plan into action. He felt sure like Sally that Meriiti had in some small part come back in Sarah, he urged Sally though to love her as Sarah and not as Meriiti, Sarah would not understand yet, if ever. Hartol began his tale again and shared brother Hughs plan and Sally's part in the plot. With caution he left out his visit to Meriiti with the Gods and Hector and the book of Moirai the less she knew the better.

REINCARNATION 1721

When Hartol first saw Tom and Sarah he knew straight away they were from another time, he knew they were special and had the gift of time travel, they were like the ancient Star Gazers and again he thought of the day he first met Meriiti and saw Sally the one who was left behind, Hartol wished he had understood more all those years ago he could have maybe saved so many things, now though he had the chance to put everything back, he could save Lacey and Billy the Centaurs and brother Hugh. He had a problem though, he had to convince both Tom and Sarah to go back in time through the waterfall. Hartol had to find brother Hugh quickly the time had come, the time they could change history and this was their last chance. He had not seen Tom or Sarah since he had run away and been saved by Sally. He worried they would no longer trust him and they would be right not to, so many things could go badly for any of them, it was going to be a hard job to persuade his friends, he maybe had no other choice than to trick them. He also had to lie, he could not tell Lacey and Billy for this plan would mean they were unlikely to ever meet and run away together from the castle, he knew they would never agree to not knowing each other as they loved each other so much. Hartol had another problem the baby Bobby, Sarah went every where with the infant it would have to be looked after by some one and the only person he knew was Sally, it was a massive risk for her, if she was to be found with the baby and Sarah and Tom could not return quickly enough, Hartol paced around the woodland as his mind reeled with so many thoughts and decisions to make, when he got back to the Dell he found Artu and so Hartol began to tell his dearest friends of his dilemmas and plots that lay ahead.

TOM & SARAH & RABBIT STEW 1721

Tom had had some hard explaining to do to his Pa, after his strange disappearance and reappearance, he of course could not mention Sally and the Dell and its mystical creatures, he instead just told what had happened, that he had runaway in such grief for his Ma, his Pa was understanding and with the funeral over and not much to do at home, he said Tom should take some time to just rest, he would send his older sister over to keep him company, Tom protested that that was not necessary he would be fine and preferred to be alone, with reluctance his Pa agreed. As soon as Tom's Pa had left for work the next morning, Tom was off across the fields to Sarah's cottage, he found her sat on the backdoor step singing to Bobby, as soon as Bobby saw Tom he gave a huge smile and giggled, Sarah went over to greet him, they quickly decided to pack up some picnic supplies and headed to the woodlands and the Dell, the wood was peaceful that morning everything was so still and little stirred the black bird did not greet them and the wind could not even muster a gentle breeze, they heard no birds and both became a little concerned by the lack of normal sounds, even little Bobby choose not to growl in his normal fashion, every step they took seemed loud on the hollow sounding path and every twig that cracked amplified across the wood, with no words their little procession continued, the only sound was the squeak of Bobby's, the path seemed longer than normal and they felt as though they were being redirected by the wood, they passed unfamiliar trees and caves they had not seen before, both became concerned and little Bobby began to growl sensing their fear. Tom and Sarah carried on though they felt sure to go back now would be harder and Tom although he would not admit it, was lost. They struggled down a rocky track and eventually came into a glade, on the edge a little wooden hut stood with smoke coming from its chimney, cups and small buckets hung on the side and dried flowers and herbs decorated the little canopy, a distinctive smell of rabbit stew drifted through the air and soon they were greeted by Sally, she looked different she seemed to glow silver, she smiled and beckoned them as though they were expected guests, Sally called them by their names, much to Sarah's relief she wasn't sure about the other strange name, they were ushered around the hut and under a glorious canopy lit with little fire flies that sparkled and darted giving a wondrous display, there was a small fire that gave off a wonderful scent and a large wooden tree trunk was elaborated with forest flowers, they were invited to sit on the big comfy moss carved logs. Once settled they were served delicious stew in bowls and given a strange sweet intoxicating drink, Sally asked them many questions about their families and she coed and giggled with Bobby, he happily growled and gurgled back, eating his bread by dipping it in his stew bowl. Sally was quite the entertainer and showed them amazing tricks she could do, she made magical fire displays and turned Eudes her Rook into a beautiful brightly coloured bird, the bird sat there talking and repeating everything everyone said, Bobby was fascinated and exhausted he slumped and slept, Tom and Sarah began to feel sleepy so Sally covered them in furs and bid them to have a sweet gentle snooze. Sarah fell into an uncanny sleep and with it she had a powerful dream, she held Tom's hand and went through the waterfall into a world where an ancient forest stretched to the end of the land and a enormous castle and cathedral burst into the sky, with the singing of angels flying on golden wings, then the darkness followed an endless abyss.

THE WOODS BACK IN TIME 1386

Sarah and Tom woke up in Sally's canopy only it seemed different it wasn't quite so elaborate and had a dull feel to it, the dawn crept with a strange light and an ear splintering chorus from the birds, they looked around and couldn't see Sally or Bobby or the strange coloured bird, instead only the black rook Eudes who pecked around eying them suspiciously, the fire flies were gone and all looked very gloomy. Sarah and Tom had a sudden panic something was very, very wrong, Sarah started to freak out and called for Bobby, tears stung her eyes as she feared the worst, they had been tricked by Sally the witch in the woods. Tom tried to calm her although inside he felt the same desperation and called for Bobby, they looked in the rackety hut and found nothing, both began to search around in disbelief they saw many animals and heard the cries of wolves in the distance, the woodland was thicker and darker, stunning wild flowers grew reaching for the sunshine, through the deep canopy above. Sarah and Tom started to search cautiously away from the hut, Sarah held back her tears in anger as she repeated Bobby's name softly. Through the glade they saw Hartol and Artu, both relieved and annoyed Tom ran to him demanding answers, Sarah followed in floods of tears, now they knew they had been tricked, both feared they were dead and ghosts like Lacey and Billy, was this the way they had met their fate, then they saw appearing through the trees a tall rounded man in a brown robe with a hood pulled over his head, he looked at their distressed states and calmed them with his gentle words, he introduced himself as brother Hugh, he told them of a new world and a time when their dear sisters and Ma wouldn't die, he told them that Lacey and Billy would live and the Centaurs would come back and the ancient woods would stretch from the sea and all over the land protecting the world, other countries would live in the same way full of woodland and hope. Tom and Sarah cared little for the woods and the world, they did not believe a word he said and insisted on answers, especially where Bobby was. Hartol wisely knew they could never see the bigger picture, how could they, he felt sad to have hurt them by tricking them, he had had no choice though, Hugh spoke again explaining why they had to do this, he said it was the only way to save the precious Dell the ancient woods and Centaurs and Fauns, Hugh then paused and looked closely at Tom and Sarah he almost whispered to them, he told them Bobby was safe with Sally she would guard him well with her life, Bobby had to stay in the future they could never risk him coming through the fountain of time. Sarah spluttered through her tears, people would come looking for them they would ruin everything that was left. Hartol proudly stepped forward he nuzzled Sarah and Tom and explained as best as he could, that it would be fine Sally had left a trail of deceit. Tom and Sarah looked at each other it was hopeless, they were stuck in a different time, trying not to scream hysterically, Tom calmly asked what an on Gods earth did Hugh think they could do, how could they change the course of the future, Hugh realising they had accepted defeat asked them to follow, they walked along the track to Hughs little pony and cart, they were introduced to Struddle who gave a little neigh and stamp of her hooves, Hugh gave her half an apple from his pocket and passed the rest to Tom and Sarah to feed her, she gladly accepted, Tom and Sarah cautiously got into the cart, they were followed by Hartol and Artu for a while, they then parted company, Tom and Sarah remained prickly, they felt betrayed and used. Hugh began to explain how things would work, on their journey along the pretty river bank. Sarah was to work along side Lacey at the monastery, they needed to become the best of friends and like wise Tom and Billy would meet in the stables at the castle, he told them the dangers of the time, they were to obey

the rules and keep their heads down. Tom still didn't understand
how any of it would help, Hugh stopped the cart and went to the
back he got out a large book, the book was decorated in jewels and
gold, he opened the book on the first page there was a picture of
the Dell the illustrations almost came to life, Sarah and Tom stared
in amazement it was as though they could have stepped onto the
page, there was a drawing of a godly figure followed by people
dressed much like Sally, Hugh read from a small chapter on the
first page. The book told off a prophecy that a god would walk the
earth, he was the god of all and would bring the world together.
Hugh then closed and carefully hid the book, Tom and Sarah
looked shocked they could all hang if this was discovered, Tom
was only young but he knew that religion was not to be argued
with. Tom was now really worried Hugh planned something bigger than he could have ever imagined. He asked how this would
happen and who would ever have the power and the capability to
make this happen. Hugh proclaimed with two words as if it was
the most obvious thing in the world, the King, he proclaimed that
the King had the power at this time with intervention, exasper-
ated he tried to explain again that the gods predicted the future
will be full of unbearable misery for so many if the course of humans was not changed. Tom and Sarah sat silently this was huge
this was beyond anything they could even imagine, afraid and
confused they maintained their silence, Hugh let them contem-
plate his outburst, understanding it was not only an impossible
task, it was also to much to take in for two children from another
century. Struddle trotted along pulling the cart without a care in
the world, the track by the river was bumpy but straight and
guided them through the valley, Sarah watched the charming coloured boats on the river, the boats were laden with baskets full of
apples, potatoes or suedes, a few times Struddle had to be pulled
over to let huge shire horses through that pulled the heavy boats
along hampered with stone or wood, the river became busy and
voices could be heard shouting and calling out their produce or
trade, some waited in carts near by ready to take stock, others just
walked along watching and listening, stalls sold food and drink

the smells and sounds hit Sarah and Tom fascinated and cautious they clung firmly to the cart. Brother Hugh waved at many as he passed, they turned up from the river through land that was more cultivated and then they saw the huge monastery that dramatically spread out and up, its wooden timbers and thatched roof spread for what seamed like miles and in construction an enormous stone building sprung from the ground masons and carpenters worked, carving, sculpting and heaving the immense structure into shape, still Hugh was silent they went through an wooden arch into a courtyard where stables with horses and carts stood waiting for their striders patiently. Tom automatically helped Hugh, while Sarah carefully dismounted, she went to fuss Struddle while the cart was emptied, Struddle's soft nuzzle pushed at Sarah for more fuss, Sarah stroked the pony chatting about the strangeness of the day as if Struddle understood, Struddle stamped his hooves and nodded his head. She helped unbridle him, Struddle followed Hugh dutifully to his little corner stall full with fresh water grain apples and hay, exhausted Struddle would be left to rest for a good few days. Tom and Sarah then followed Hugh he took them into a huge garden fenced off with high timbers, he hid the book in his cabin and then took them into the monastery, the other monks seemed not to notice Sarah and Tom, he spoke with another brother who eyed them cautiously, Hugh had a sham tale to tell him, they were then lead to separate dormitories low and dark they smelt stale and felt cold, each had neat cots side by side, Sarah felt panic to be separated from Tom her sense told her though Hugh would let no harm come to them, to him they were precious. Sarah changed into the clothes laid out on the bed, they were scratchy so she put her own dress back on underneath, she then followed Hugh who had reappeared with Tom in his plain robes, they went into what she presumed was a school room, some boys sat at small tables and watched the monk who wrote letters on a large slate, he would tirelessly come around to each individual and quietly sound out the letter and help them to write it on their small slate, they made their marks in white stone and all that could be heard in the vaulted room was the scratch marks and whispers from the monk, the next room was a work room where others did tasks of mending robes or weaving fabrics, Sarah noticed Lacey straight away her amazing long blond hair, blue eyes and rosy skin were all brighter, Sarah was sat next to her at a loom and without words their smile shared was a bond for life. Tom was fascinated by the silent school watched and learnt in silence, while Sarah was left to try and follow Lacey with her quick work on the intricate loom. Later they followed the others to prayer and then to a huge hall where all sat in silence eating a humble meal of potato with small amounts of some meat and a watery broth, they then had a huge bowl of stewed apple with a sweet bread flavoured with elderflower and a strange spice, they were taken to the dormitory afterwards and as the light had left the sky in silence they all lay down for sleep, Lacey and Sarah were the only young girls in the dormitory, a couple of older girls came in a little later who were nuns their silence unbroken. Sarah lay in silence and fear, she found sleep hard to find, her head was reeling she worried for Bobby and her parents, Sarah missed her safe cottage by the wood and she could not think how they could help in Hughs unthinkable plan, she felt anxious and was terrified she would never escape this place of silence.

MORNING CALL 1386

Sarah was woken by Lacey and she bid her to follow her, quickly dressing and washing from the warm water that ran under the stones and into a natural bowl, Sarah followed her impatient leader still in silence, they went out through a tiny door that lead into the kitchen gardens, here they could quietly talk and picking up a basket like Lacey, Sarah asked quietly what they were to do, Lacey eyed her suspiciously asking how she knew her name, Sarah fumbled an answer that Hugh had told her, easily convinced Lacey smiled and said she liked brother Hugh, he was kind and she told Sarah about the Abbot who was nasty and told her which monks to keep clear of, they carefully picked the tiny strawberries placing them in the baskets on the cloth, the job was fiddly and time consuming Sarah did not care though it was lovely to have the sunshine on her face and the sweet company of Lacey, Lacey told her lots about the monastery and that she was an orphan like the others, Lacey presumed Sarah was an orphan and she thought Tom was her brother, so Sarah let her think this without saying much. Sarah then saw brother Hugh with Tom he walked with his arms in prayer and spoke to Tom in his whispers the plot had begun and Sarah knew it was serious, Tom didn't lift his head to look at her, his daunted pale face concentrated on what Hugh told him, Sarah knew he was going to the castle soon, she wished dearly she could tell Lacey all about Billy, Sarah knew now though that they were never to meet, Lacey would not go to the castle, she would continue her lessons and work in the monastery and become a nun or serf, she would never roam freely with Billy and Sarah could not decide in her own head, if that was better that she lived along life here in the confound's of the monastery or was she better to have a short care free life with an innocent young love, it was not Sarah's choice, brother Hugh she felt was certainly playing God and this was his second chance to get it right or wrong. Lacey saw her concern and bid she hurried with her picking they had still more work to do, Sarah tried to wave or something to Tom before she left the garden, he avoided her though and Sarah reluctantly followed Lacey in doors and was lead to the kitchen, where they washed the fruit and poured jugs of wine over it and mixed it with finely ground almonds this was mixed and left, after carefully washing the seeds from their hands in the bubbling warm spring waters, Sarah followed Lacey to morning prayers followed by a breakfast of bread and milk, Sarah's days would remain the same, each day would be full of prayers, lessons, chores and mainly silence, it was clear only a few privileged were aloud freedom like brother Hugh. Sarah took comfort in Lacey and a little plan of her own started to form in her mind, if brother Hugh was to play with the worlds future and past, Sarah thought maybe she could also make a little harmless adjustments. Sarah mulled these thoughts over at night in the quiet of the monastery, all she heard was the scamper of rats and cries from the owls, she listened more carefully and convinced no monk wandered the halls at night, Sarah decided to creep out to Hugh's cabin, something about the book he had hidden intrigued her, she saw it in her thought's and heard a strange language, she saw the people like Sally and she saw herself as one of them in her vivid imagination, Sarah slipped through the garden door leaving it slightly a jar, she walked in the shadows of the fruit bushes and carefully made her way to the cabin, she found the key she had seen Hugh hide in the rhubarb pot and as quietly as possible opened the door, the most unlikely place to hide something was a manure sack and sure enough carefully wrapped in hessian, it sat in a sack full of hay, below the stinking horse manure, Sarah hesitantly sat in the corner on the floor and opened the book, she recognised the pages and pictures that came to life, Sarah now knew that Sally was right, Sarah somehow had been here before long ago in the crystal pool and this scripture once lost had now found itself in the hands of a simple monk, with an unbelievable mission, Sarah heard a noise and quickly hid the book, she locked the door and replaced the key, then practically crawled back to the door, she clung to the shadows and looked back to see the strangest of sights, a tall monk stood with long white hair and piercing eyes, he prayed to the skies and then he looked straight at Sarah and knelt, Sarah panicked and ran back to her dormitory, she quickly got under her sparse itchy blanket and closed her eyes, she saw the flicker of a candle and heard voices. They looked for someone, Sarah lay terrified she had been seen and became more worried that she had given the secret of the book away. Did the strange monk plan to take the book of scripture, Sarah agonised over what she had done, she lay like a statue that night listening to every sound, she heard and saw a light flash over her and Lacey, still they searched for their intruder, Sarah sensed none would be found, the godly monk was no doubt long gone.

AN IMPORTANT GUEST RICHARD OF BORDEAUX 1386

Tom and Hugh arrived at Farleigh castle as the rest of the world seemed to, the afternoon was bright and the castle towered across the valley, They rode through the castle gates on horse back after taking the river track from the monastery in Bath, the track had been busy full of carts, farmers and merchants bringing goods to the castle, their arrival was of no importance and the guards on the gate ushered brother Hugh and his assistant through quickly, today they had no time for idle chatter with the monk, Hugh carried the ancient scripture in a sack bag that crossed over his chest and was hidden by the folds of his habit and cloak, Tom wore the same habit and cloak and the two monks headed straight to the small chapel, they lit the incense and prayed for the safe arrival of the King, Hugh was to hold morning prayers for the Hungerford family before the arrival of their very important guest, Thomas Hungerford hoped to talk to King Richard and bend his ear for his own political gains. Hugh knew of this political outrage through gossip and hoped dearly his quest would cease more greed and damage. Hugh purposefully had planned his sermon and prayers with words that would ring out selfless acts for personal benefits and how obeying God and the king was the only hope of salvation. The Hungerford's arrived dressed in their finery, Hugh quietly tutted at such extravagances, while Tom watched them in amazement, these people were fine and imposing and he prayed that their plan worked, he was certain if not, he would definitely not make it out alive or in one piece, he could tell they cared little for Hugh's words to them it was merely a formality, they had a demure of callous arrogance. Tom thought of Sarah and hoped she was managing, he could not look at her for a second that morning, afraid he would grab her and run with her to where he had no clue. Tom calmed himself and with relief brother Hugh's dull prayers were over, they followed the small procession out into the court yard, where small chit chat was performed then everyone quickly disappeared in anticipation of their arriving guest. The courtyard bustled, serfs, guards and courtiers fled in all directions, so a young monk was of no suspicion, as he entered the castle holding holy water and incense with his humble cross sack bag, he followed the instructions to the Kings quarters, where he performed his task of blessing the room for the occupant, no one would ever think or suspect that when brother Hugh left that he left alone, a forgotten detail and of no concern. Tom was now left in the Kings large room of the castle he watched, Hugh from the slit windows as he rode through the gates with no back ward glance, Tom settled in his hiding place he opened the large ancient book and began to read its words, Tom was not sure why but felt as though the book had a hold over him it was as though the pages turned themselves and the words sprung of the pages and the illustrations seemed almost to come to life he felt pain and fear and smelt the smells, the words in another language should have made no sense yet he read and understood most, he could not stop staring at the detailed paintings, he saw the Fauns and what he presumed were the Centaurs he saw Hartol and someone that reminded him of Sally and Sarah, he saw the fountain and crystal pool, so immersed Tom barely noticed the hours pass and the commotion grow outside. The King Richard of Bordeaux and his huge trail of couriers, soldiers and serfs strode through the gates, he travelled with his beloved wife Anne of Bohemia with her ladies in waiting. Tom heard the distant sounds, yet he was still absorbed in the book he continued to look and with each page he felt stronger and more sure of Hugh's crusade, the words he could understand were like songs that stayed in his mind and he saw the predictions, the death the ruin and the devastation of the world in the glorious art, the gods showed another way, away of peace. Tom snapped out of his dream like trance and grew very nervous when he heard the voices on the stone steps, he heard the clang of weapons and the roar from the guard, as a serf was chastised for being in the wrong place, the door to the chamber opened and the King stepped in, only ten years older than Tom, King Richard looked much wiser for his years, from his hidden spot he saw the servants tend to his every need, they were then dismissed and just as Hugh had said, the King slept full of fine food and good wine. Tom quietly crept from the hidden whole in the wall and gently stepped to the side of the Kings bed and as if to a sleeping child, he opened the scripture, he described the pictures and said the words he could, then Tom started speaking in a language he did not know and his voice became more powerful and felt more like a spell, Tom felt as though he was in a dream and saw moving knights in white armour circling and a god like figure in the pictures of the book came alive and the story of all the horrors, wonders, tragedies and evolution told the story both harrowing and splendid, intoxicating and suffocating the book did its work as dawn broke, the book had come to its end . Tom hid in his hidden humble hole, Tom watched and saw something he would never forget or quite believe the white knights still circled and each one evaporated and in wisps, then a figure like a King from another time rose, Tom glimpsed his piercing eyes and godly figure as he joined the air, the King would breathed in deeply and the spirits were gone, Tom saw with his eyes the King change ever so slightly, he looked stronger and kinder, wiser and more godly. Tom was unsure quite what had just happened but the King of this time he believed was no longer a mere mortal, he was a god who walked the earth and his presence was captivating beyond belief. Tom sat firmly in astonishment and fear, he knew he had to stay for the plan to work, the book had to stay hidden the words could never be undone. Tom exhausted slept he curled into a tiny ball and later when he heard the horses hooves and the trumpets blow, he carefully moved to the window hiding the book and spreading incense as he went and praying, Tom again moved freely around the castle, its cold stone walls would thankfully only capture him for a short time, relieved he walked out into the fresh air, away from the stale smell of smoke fires, boiled food and ale, he found the stable yard easily and as promised he saw Billy, Tom felt like hugging him he was so relieved to see his once ghostly friend, now larger than life, with bouncy curls and freckles he grinned at Tom eager to set off, Billy as instructed by brother Hugh had saddled two ponies and he would accompany Tom back to the monastery, they were to take the long way through the woods, avoiding passers by and questions. Both trotted off quickly, Tom was not used to riding, thankfully though he had had a couple of goes on his uncles mine pony called Pebbles, these ponies were similar to Pebbles in many ways they had sturdy bodies and thick grey fur, yet they were agile and frisky after a long night in the stables with plenty of fodder. Billy guided them quickly to the cover of the woods and led them of onto small paths, made by fallow deer or other woodland creatures, the woods were quiet and felt safe, both kept their whits though not knowing quite what they could meet, the wood became strangely familiar to Tom and even with hundreds of years yet to pass, he could sense where he was, the river lay to his left and the valley rose to the right, the sun that crept through the branches, Tom sensed they were now not so far from the Dell, his mind began to reel could he escape and just head back alone hoping this would speed up Sarah's return. Tom's manic thoughts were interrupted by Billy who hissed at him to follow quickly, they fled down a tiny track barely big enough for the ponies to squeeze through the thicket, with their heads down soothing the ponies, they both stayed as still as possible and listened, Tom watched in horror as an army of centaurs half horse half man thundered past, their leader shouted orders and it was not long before both Billy, Tom and the ponies were flushed out from the thicket, not sure what to say or make of their capturers both kept their heads down and prayed for some intervention to save them.

A FRIENDSHIP FOREVER 1386

Sarah had immersed herself in monastery life, she enjoyed her lessons and learnt quickly, she spent time in the infirmary learning how to heel and mix potions, her limited knowledge of the future, strangely helped her earn respect as she would insist on cleanliness and fresh air, Sarah ripped old fabrics and made masks for the monks who attended the sick, explaining this would help stop them getting the disease, these facts she had learnt from the dreadful Mother Darcy, unlike Lacey, Sarah was not afraid of some of the monks and even the Abbot who was she agreed a sly one, she felt he was no worse than the master of the hall her Pa and Ma worked for, he was just selfish and narrow minded, she avoided him and pleased him with her gracious curtseys and politeness, Lacey being bright and demure copied her new friend and the two became popular and more respected for young girls, they would gather wild flowers whilst out walking and decorate parts of the monastery, Sarah taught Lacey how to make scones and jam that they served to the monks, when the prior was away, they would sing little songs that Sarah knew, Sarah and Lacey decorated their little dormitory making it sweet with the smell of lavender and blossom, Sarah made the best of her situation at night she would pray for Tom, he had been gone for longer than he should have been, Hugh reassured her though he was no longer at the castle, he just feared they had become lost on their journey back to the monastery, Hugh was unable to investigate until the Abbot had left for London, so they patiently waited, Hugh prayed for Tom, he also prayed for his plan to have worked, he had heard that the King had summoned the Abbots and gentry across the land, other rumours circulated of the Kings godly appearance, his excitement for success was hard to contain and every time he saw Sarah's concerned sweet face, he felt guilt for using them in a such a way, but glad it may have worked. Hugh was amazed by her composure and effort to please and learn, he complimented her and tried his hardest to make her time in the monastery bearable, never dare he though mention her dear little Bobby, this he knew was too much for her to contain. Finally the day arrived and with some preparation and many instructions, the Abbot left the safe walls of the monastery, with its steaming spa's and fresh springs of water, he left behind the sweet orchards and herb gardens for the streets of London with their filth and crowds, Hugh could see his reluctance to leave and felt no pity as he vanished from sight. Without any hesitation he had Struddle tacked with his harness to the cart and was about to leave, when he saw Sarah and Lacey running with their cloaks and little cloth bags, Sarah blurted, she had told brother William they had been instructed by the Abbot to assist in searching for woodland herbs, Hugh shook his head in frustration, with little negotiation and not wanting to draw attention he helped the girls up, Sarah was annoying with her cleverness, Hugh had no choice but to take them, with no words they headed for the river and the bridge, Hugh needed to find Hartol quickly, he knew he could help find Tom and the answer's he so desperately needed. The small party sat quietly in the cart and disappeared from the monastery, all believed that they were off in search of herbs, what else would brother Hugh ever do, respected and loved for his extensive gardening knowledge the monks encouraged his work and travels in the Abbots absence. The monastery would once again become relaxed with a few strict rules broken, silence was one and a favoured game of boule broke out within hours, laughter and mild chatter could be heard in the cloisters. The morning was fair and of late Hugh had noticed the weather was generally kind, his mind would constantly drift to the book and sermons Tom had unwittingly read, if the King had become possessed by the Gods and

Knights as the scripture in the book foretold, then soon the world would surely become a different place, he felt nervous that he had changed his precious life, maybe he would regret his actions, he had seen the future though and he had never carried it out for his own self preservation, he thought of the book and how he would like to hold it and turn its beautiful pages once more, he would like to see the paintings that came to life and hear the voices in his head of the Gods. Lacey and Sarah broke his trance of deep thoughts, both let out a small squeal of fear, they had travelled far into the woods and on an abandoned track in the depths, they heard the thundering hooves approach before they could turn or see their pursuers, Hugh held is breath and prayed to God as poor Struddle whinnied in fear.

BOBBY AND HIS CART 1721

The villagers had searched the woods and fields for the missing, Tom, Sarah and little Bobby, it was all to much with so much loss already, they seemed to fear the worse the sherif was called, still no evidence or trace could be found, it was as though they had vanished into thin air, not a track or clue could be found and soon the search stopped and they just waited in limbo with little hope. Both of Sarah and Tom's Pa were out every free hour they had, Sarah's Pa was sure they had drowned and been taken by the river, no other explanation fitted, still they would look though, they found the woods an eerie and unwelcome place to be and often they would return home with an uneasy feeling that something watched them, so often they felt a presence and glimpsed a movement and heard a crack of twigs, they began to feel suspicious and believed in the strange happenings in Brown Folly Woods, many started to make reports of sightings on the track, a carriage had turned in fear of a ghostly apparition of a young girl in white and the sightings became more frequent and the woods a more futile place, some would gossip that it was the ghosts of Sarah and Tom, this idle chatter and whisperings would break out into fights and fear, the village became an unfriendly place, no children roamed and doors became locked, the once gentle sermons in church took on a sombre note and warning of evil and of casting out demons. It was not long before a witch hunt had begun with so many rumours and tales, with three missing children and the strange disappearance of Tom once before, they suspected a coven grew in the woods and one misty morning there were pitch forks at dawn, as the farmers, gardeners, poachers, gamekeepers and all set out to find the lost souls and living tormentors. Hartol, Artu and Sally had all seen this momentum grow they knew danger was approaching, the morning the villagers mobbed together, their plan was simple and a little strange, however the villagers would be offset by the move, buying them precious time as brothers Hugh's plan unfolded hundreds of years before. As the armed crowd approached the woodland track that lead down into the woods it became covered in a thick swirling mist, they would see before them through the trees, the ghost of a boy simply dressed and the ghost of girl all in white, both pushed the rackety cart and inside was little Bobby who coed and growled, pointing and giggling at his ghostly help, Sally watched over cautiously, she wanted no harm to come to the little boy, afraid they may react strangely to this apparition, she was already hiding above in the tree canopy ready to grab him, Lacey and Billy were ready to vanish and leave little Bobby. Sally sensed something was wrong Bobby grew grizzly as he saw the crowd of adults and weapons, he was scared and needed Sally or Sarah, Bobby had grown fond of his new little life, Sally adored him and gave him every second of her time. The crowd entering the woods became hesitant at first relived to see the little party, they then realised something was very wrong, they did not see Sarah and Tom but ghosts and Bobby began to scream as if possessed, in panic a local farmers boy threw a pitch fork towards the screaming infant, afraid it was the devil in disguise, without warning the pitch fork flew through the air, it fell short of Bobby in his rackety cart, Sally could take no risks, the wall of mist thickened and Bobby was gone, the cart sat empty on the woodland track with the pitch fork in front, the sinister image bought wails and fear and no one went in pursuit of the screaming infant, even his parents, uncles and aunts fled the scene, the cart was left alone on the track and the woods were boarded up with signs of a red cross clumsily painted in madder root, no one was to enter Brown Folly Woods, The village folk did not talk of the fantamasgoria of that day. Sarah's Ma and Pa quickly moved away and their cottage lay empty cursed and avoided by passers bye. Tom's Pa would stay and still search the woods from time to time with Buster the brave by his side, all he got was swirling mists and eerie creeks, no birds sang, and he felt the presence of others around, he knew he was watched and he watched back, in his heart he knew that something had happened and it was not what the villagers thought, he felt sure Tom, Sarah and Bobby were still alive he felt their thoughts and love, he would never speak to any other of his feelings that they were somewhere close, yet somehow far away. Hartol and Sally would watch Tom's Pa from a far, they let him wander freely and only drove him from the Dell and Sally's hovel, they felt sad for him seeing his pain, they sensed though he understood a concept beyond his own ability, they could only hope that what they planned would spare him more pain and his past would be so different, to the one he had already lived.

BOBBY IN THE WOODS 1721

Bobby had screamed his little heart out when he saw the crowd he was terrified and as the pitch fork hurtled towards him and Lacey and Billy disappeared, he felt the warm strong arms of Sally whisk him to the skies, the crowd vanished in the mists and he silenced himself eventually, nuzzling into the folds of Sally's cloak, they landed back at the hovel deep in the forest and exhausted Sally lay him in the cot she had made and sang gently to him stroking his forehead, he smiled and drifted to sleep, exhausted and stressed by the failure to return Bobby to his family and worried by the outcome of their failed plan, Sally paced up and down, deciding wether she should flee with Bobby or not, she was scared they would track her down and kill them both, she muttered away to herself, whilst fiddling with her beads around her neck, her ramblings were interrupted by the familiar call from Hartol and a loud stamp of his hooves as he approached. Sally went out to great him he also felt distraught by their failure and feared as Sally did an invasion of the woods, after great deliberation they decided to hold tight and use the woodland and Dell for their protection, Sally would move to the Dell for her and Bobby's safety and they would keep vigil on the woods and any visitors, they were to become an unwelcome place, guarded by ancient spells and spirits. The woods would become known as the most haunted in the land, both villagers and travellers avoided the track through Brown Folly Woods, folk wood go miles out of their way, the villagers that lived by the woods eerie silence, either moved on or stayed well away from the little tracks that lead to the woods, Warleigh Manor took on different woods for game and hunting, all lived in fear, strangely even the law did not investigate any more, the woods and disappearance of the children became a subject that was taboo. Bobby and Sally set up in the Dell by the crystal pool, Sally slept soundly with Bobby purring by her side, they spent their days paddling, fishing, foraging and playing, Bobby continued his strange growl and Sally decided little Bobby was of a special nature and not quite all he seemed, she began to realise that he needed her help more and more, the world of the village and its stubborn ways would have been hard for his temperament and sensitive persona, he grew and acted more like a puppy with each day, happy Sally let this be. Hartol seemed temporarily relaxed too, he had got what he wished for, so while he waited for the return of Tom and Sarah, he pondered on how things would change if Hugh's plan came true. If not Hartol knew in time people would forget the tales of the woodlands ghosts and stories would be hidden deep in the grave. The people and their relentless progression of destruction would be back in time and Hartol knew one day it would be a disaster for the woodlands and Dell.

THE CENTUARS 1386

Tom and Billy were held captive in the Dell, Tom knew it was the same place it just seemed different, the crystal pool was brighter and the waterfall more magnificent, glistening caves and trees stretched up to the heavens and surrounded its peaceful location, the mythical Centaurs paraded around, Tom thought the Centaurs were very grand, he at first was terrified of them and thought they had met their fate, they however only showed suspicion to Tom and Billy and treated them with kindness, although they were still their prisoners and parole did not seem an option until they found answers, Tom was afraid to tell them anything, not sure if it was the correct thing to do, he kept his secret mission to himself, although this lengthened their captivity and Tom saw no end, Billy seemed to be taking his capture well and enjoyed bathing in the pool and the waterfall, he was a very proficient tree climber and came down one day with a huge piece of honeycomb sticky and sweet, the boys guzzled it with great pleasure, they lived of the forest and waited in silence. Bauta was the leader of the fine herd of Centaurs and he spoke calmly with an air of royalty, he seemed to enjoy human contact and sought knowledge from both boys, gradually a relationship grew and the boys would have the joy of a ride through the huge woodland at a terrifying pace, the trees and ground thundered past them in a flash, the power of the Centaurs was breath taking and beautiful. The days turn to a week and Tom began fear that they would be stuck with the Centaurs forever, he thought of escape but knew it was futile, so he bided his time quietly and with each day he became closer to Billy and he began too confide in him with little snippets of his tale, Billy was surprisingly open to his late night stories and listened with a thirst for more and more, one evening as always when Tom saw the Centaurs sleeping he began his tale, this time he told Billy the tale of when he was in the castle walls and how brother Hugh and him had tricked them, he told him of his hiding place in the Kings quarters and he told him of the magic book, the book that would change the way people would live for centuries to come, he told Billy there would be no wars or plaques, forgetting Billy didn't no his future was to die of the plaque with Lacey, he then carefully avoided the subject and told Billy of how the Centaurs would be saved and the vast woodlands, eventually the world itself would be safe from the dreadful future that lay a head. Billy looked in awe at his young friend, Billy also whispered he should not breath any of this to another living soul or they would all hang high from the castle gates, Tom agreed saying it was a dangerous business and he feared he would never be free to go home and would never see Sarah and little Bobby. Billy lightened the mood by laughing, he said he would like to meet Bobby who thought he was a pup, the boys spoke late in whispers and finally not long before dawn slept, with the last of the moon seeping through the branches of the ancient trees. In the morning they woke to a commotion the Centaurs were all in formation and looked ready for battle, Bauta came over to the sleepy eyed boys and bid them maybe if they had not whispered the night away with tales, they would rise earlier and understand the reason for such behaviour, Tom gasped a little afraid Bauta had heard his tale and Bauta's looked told him all, of course the Centaur had eaves dropped to every word he said from the first night he spilled his story, Tom hung his head in disbelief he had betrayed the course, Bauta though laughed and told him he had found brother Hugh, his cart was lost on the eastern wood, Bauta gestured he joined them and soon the boys were galloping through the woods, in search of their freedom and brother Hugh.

THE AMBUSH 1386

Sarah would later that evening confide in Tom, if she had not seen him on the back of the strange beast half human, half horse she would have died of fright, they looked so huge and powerful, no one would believe they stood a chance, yet no sooner had the herd surrounded them, from their dramatic and terrifying ambush, the giants with snorting nostrils, fiery eyes and monster physics, turned to gentle gracious giants, as soon as they saw Hugh and little Struddle, they purred like cats by a winters fire, Sarah was intrigued by them, they reminded her of Artu and Arrietta, Sarah had had pangs of sadness, it made her think of Bobby and Sally and she just wanted to be back in Brown Folly Woods, with Tom in their own time, she wanted to be walking back to her cottage, the holly hocks would all be flowering now and the lovely rose bushes, her Pa had taken cuttings of from the Manor house, their perfect pink petals perfumed the air and scent pots for months, Sarah thought of her Ma who was so sad, thick tears crumbled down her cheeks and she was lost, Lacey bought her back at that moment with a gentle pat and reassurance, Tom dismounted and ran to her seeing her fear and Billy joined them, Sarah was jolted from her sadness as she realised, that the boy stood next to Tom was Billy in the flesh, their ghostly Billy was bright and fresh with his charming smile, curls and freckles, his bright blue eyes lit up when he saw Lacey and from that minute; whatever Hugh had wished to happen; Billy and Lacey had met. The impressive and humble group moved on through the dark wood, Struddle picked up her pace and pranced eagerly behind the Centaurs, the unknown paths took them deep into the woodland. When they arrived at the

Dell, Sarah like Tom would find it similar yet grander, Lacey was
dumb struck never had she seen or believed anything so magical
existed, Seeing her elated face made Sarah and Tom smile, remem-
bering their own fascination, when they first found the Dell in
their Brown Folly Woods, tears returned to Sarah and Tom held
her hand feeling her pain, they watched as Billy and Lacey drank
the waters and the group of four wandered the Dell, Sarah and
Tom each quietly contemplated their thoughts, that would later
transpire to be the same. When they came back to the main part of
the Dell and waterfall they saw Hartol he stood there in all his
grandness with Artu, Bauta and Hugh, Hugh looked small and in-
significant next to the grand gracious creatures, Tom and Sarah
knew however he was more than just a simple monk, it was no accident he had been the chosen custodian for the book, or that he
had travelled through the fountains of time. The strange group
talked for many hours and soon sleep would take over the younger
group of four. When they woke they were bobbing along in the
cart with Struddle snorting and sniffing at the dewy dawn, the
night had passed and Hugh had carefully placed each of them fast
asleep in the cart covering them in hessian, Tom woke first and
felt nervous he scrambled up and managed to take a seat at the
front next to Hugh, the others slowly woke, to hear Tom asking
many questions, about what was happening at home and how the
plan would work here and how Sarah and him wanted to go back,
frustratingly they were met with silence from Hugh and for a
while they had to ignore his strange reluctance to talk. Sarah
talked to Lacey and Billy as if it was the most normal thing in the
world to be sat in a cart, going to a monastery four hundred years
before she was even born, with two children who she knew would
die of the black death and she would meet them as ghosts, in the
woods by her cottage that she called home. Sarah thought about
Sally and how she had called her that name and Sarah became
more convinced, that maybe she did have some powers of her
own, this woman Meriiti who ever she was must have been special, Sally knew about so many tricks and potions, maybe Sarah
would try a little spell herself and although Sarah's mind was full

of so many different thoughts, she managed to carry on chatting, she felt it was reassuring, so she babbled on admiring the morning and its beauty and loving the company of her dear friends Billy and Lacey, she looked at Tom who looked strong and proud and somehow different than before something about him had changed, Sarah desperately wanted to ask him all about the book and the King and tell him how she thought that they had to do something to help themselves and their friends, brother Hugh had bigger fish to fry. She sensed they were of little use to him now.

THE BIGGER FISH 1386

Brother Hugh felt bad for blatantly ignoring Tom's flow of questions, he had every entitlement to know the answers, for now though Hugh had no answers, he only had questions himself, he needed to understand how the King had been effected by the book and what his part would be, he needed some evidence of success, before he could let the children go, Hugh could not accept failure he had waited to long he knew this was his last chance. If he had to send Tom back to the King in this century he would. He sat in his modest room that looked out over the pretty and productive walled garden, he wished he had had a simple life of herbs and such, had he not met Arrietta and Sally and the return of Meriiti, then he would most probably be like the other monks, with no care but to study, serve God and fill their bellies with as much as they could away from the Abbots watchful eye. Hugh though had to face his responsibility, he believed it to be the most important of the Lord God's work ever to be done, he just happened to be the vessel of the deed. Hugh reached under his bed and found his locked wooden box in there he had a rough copy of the book, he had taken the precaution to copy each prayer and sermon and he had copied the wonderful pictures, although his scruffy sketches bore little resemblance to the true ones in the book, his scribbles still illustrated what he needed to remember, the real book was now well hidden in the rocks of the waterfall of time. Hugh found parts of the book were in Sanskrit a language he had never mastered, He thought of brother Eymen he was once an extensive traveller and he had once heard him speak to another of his knowledge of many languages including Sanskrit, he would ask him for a translation, Hugh took the carefully copied script. After evening prayer Hugh approach brother Eymen, the tall proud man from faraway was no longer dark haired and strong as he had once been, he was now silver and frail, yet he still had his smouldering dark eyes and the kindest smile, he greeted Hugh with pleasure and with enthusiasm when he was set a challenge, Eymen proclaimed his mind was a little slow after his evening super and prayer so asked to keep the drawings and writings, Hugh had supposedly been given by a fellow monk who passed by on his travels, Hugh thanked him graciously and returned to his room, where he continued to study the book and it was then that it struck him, once he had gained the final translation the missing piece, with such knowledge of the book, he must find his way to the King, he could surely be the best advisor, frustrated and impatient for the translation he tossed and turned the night away, after many hours of broken sleep, with relief at last he heard the bell chime for prayer, Hugh tried to remain calm and perceive he had no rush for the translations, so he went to the garden after prayers and began to work, neglected by his absence the weeds had begun to take hold, he hoed and scratched at the earth in haste, knowing Eymen would translate his words in his own time, Eymen would as always stroll through the cloisters and sit by his favourite lavender bushes, from there he would see brother Hugh as he toiled in his garden, this for Hugh was the quickest way he knew of persuading brother Eymen to work quickly without a word of encouragement. As predicted Eymen sat with his books and slate and looked to see Hugh, then set forth to work with no break of a potter or morning mead. Whilst Hugh waited and worked himself, Sarah and Lacey came into the gardens to fetch herbs and fruits for the meals of the day, not wanting to be bombarded with questions he ignored them and carried on with his work, they in turn ignored Hugh in the same way and filled their baskets and bowls with little chatter, Hugh felt Sarah's eyes upon him though, he felt her presence and once he caught her stare, he saw a different stronger and more self assured Sarah starring at him through those soft brown eyes, Hugh shook his head, he went to the spring and drank water to clear his head, to his relief when he turned back Sarah and Lacey had gone to the kitchens, brother Eymen approached him with his kind smile, waving the paper, he told Hugh it made no sense at all and laughed, he thought maybe his monk he had met, had had one to one many a bibble on his journey. Hugh graciously thanked him and laughed at his comments, agreeing he was a strange monk that he had met, he chatted to Eymen about the weather and ways of the world, Hugh thanked him again and casually wandered to his room as if he had not a care in the world, whilst inside Hugh's heart raced like a drum, he hadn't even looked at the papers not wishing to seem to eager, Hugh carefully placed them on his desk he drew back the wooden shutters letting the sun shine into his room and began to read the translation, the scripture told of a god who would walk on the earth until he found the human who could hold the book of Moirai the book of fates, he immediately thought of Hector overwhelmed Hugh greedily read on, he knew enough to know the three names were those of the mythical Gods, he needed to read up on the names in the great library, before that though Hugh went to prayer and then ate, at super he felt the stares of the children, he avoided them as he did others glances and kept himself to himself, afraid he would give something away. Later in the library he researched in secret the three greek goddess's Clotho, Lachesis and Atropos each would decide the fates of all, Clotho would spin the thread of life, Lachesis would cut the thread to the type of life and Atropos would decide upon the length of life and death. The words in the book started to make sense, each reading was a command of each destiny and the Gods wished to control the destiny of the world, they had been over thrown long ago, the book of Moirai was lost and the legends were forgotten, man on earth alone determined destiny and although he could still not choose his death, his life works he could change and this was what the Gods wished for, not to destroy the humans or stop their religious and cultural beliefs, but to stop the humans destructive destiny. Hugh was more than satisfied he now understood. He again thought of Hector with his unearthly and godly ways, he felt certain now Hugh was truly the chosen one. He would make haste in the morning to Shrewsbury Castle, he knew King Richard would be there to hold council at the Abbey. Hugh's shutters slammed back and forth, a strong wind had grown from nowhere, the wind was warm and swirled across the land, wrapping around both man and beast a firm and gentle touch and heady sweetness was left hanging in the air, a sign the Gods were preparing for this momentous shift in time.

THE ESCAPE WITH A STRUDDLE 1386

Tom and Sarah had both had enough of Hugh's silence, they no longer trusted him and saw he was possessed with his work, they knew without his help that they would have to wait to leave, until he had solved whatever he needed to solve, they however did not know how long this could take, they saw him at supper distancing himself on the long trestle tables, he clung to the shadows of the monasteries corners, they watched him disappear into the huge library and knew they were lost in this time, as Hugh choose to ignore then, Tom and Sarah decided to do something about it. Tom signalled to Sarah discreetly to follow and thankfully as always she understood him with so little effort, they both went in different directions and met in the walled garden, Sarah had grabbed a basket and Tom a bucket full of water, whilst appearing to do chores on opposites sides of the blackberry bushes, they started their perilous chat, they both agreed on so many things quickly and saw no option but to escape and with little discussion, they had both already decided that they would take Billy and Lacey, Tom arranged they would meet down by the river meadows at dawn, he urged Sarah not to forget a thing they would not be back, both scurried back in unnoticed, Sarah placed her blackberries ready for the morning and went to find Lacey, they had a few chores to do before bed, Sarah decided not to tell Lacey a thing she would be to nervous and couldn't possibly understand anything that was about to happen and had happened, that night Sarah tossed and turned afraid of so many things that could go wrong,

Sarah calmed herself, she had to have her head screwed on for the next day and she thought of Artu, Arrietta and Hugh who had all travelled between the times, Sarah knew the fountain was the access point she was unsure how it worked though, she felt sure the Centaurs would know the way, could they trick them into thinking it was brother Hugh's wishes to show them how. Sarah only managed a little restless sleep in the itchy bed, with relief a tiny light shone from the skies, she was ready to leave, she had packed both of their meagre belongings into small cloth bags, she gently woke Lacey telling her they had orders from Hugh, they left the dim dormitory and headed for the kitchens, Sarah picked up the basket of blackberries, quickly adding a loaf of yesterdays bread, turning she looked at the monastery kitchen with its huge colanders and fire pits, she looked at the straw floor and wooden walls, with wonderful clay pots, jugs, bowls and huge cooking vessels, she thought of the vast library and the eating halls, the wonderful cloisters and carvings, the gardens and beautiful abbey, with its wonderful arches and beautiful decoration, she savoured each moment and all the monks with their unique characteristics and knowledge, she then turned on her bare heel, grabbing Lacey's hand she challenged her to race to the river meadow, Lacey giggled and ran as Sarah guilty ran by her side; Brother Eymen watched the girls run, he smiled to himself a memory stirred of his long lost sister and Mother running with him flying a kite, he could remember the stony mountains and hot sands, a tear escaped his old eyes, yet he smiled again as the girls disappeared into the meadows long grass, Eymen would turn a blind eye, youth was a wonderful thing under a dawn sky. Lacey squealed with joy as she ran into the meadow and saw Tom and Billy, Sarah relieved ran harder as if chased by a wolf, confused she saw Struddle tied to his cart happily munching the sweet meadow grass, Tom shrugged it was the only way, Billy and Lacey happily boarded and Billy took the reins both convinced by their dear friends, that they were under the orders of Hugh, Struddle happily trotted along the familiar river track they crossed the bridge and entered the woodland path, deer, badgers and foxes crisscrossed the well trodden tracks, little field mice ran from the carts tumbling wheels, the rabbits sat nibbling their early breakfast of groundsel and dandelions, while the birds tweeted their ever songs, never before had Tom and Sarah heard so many birds sing so loudly, the small group of friends sat in silence while they watched and listened to the wonders of the woods, knowing the deeper they got that the Centaurs would soon be upon them. Although this was scary at the time it was the one thing they desperately needed, Struddle seemed to know the way so Billy let him have a free rein to take them deeper into the woods, they had been travelling for no more than an hour, when they heard the terrifying sound as the Centaurs approached and no sooner had they heard them they were they surrounded, Sarah gasped not with fear of the Centaurs, but in fear of what they were about to do.

AN UNLIKELY AGREEMENT 1721

Sally paced the woods as she cuddled Bobby to sleep in her arms, he had a slight fever and Sally knew that was not good, she took him to the cool waters of the crystal pond, as she concentrated on Bobby, Hartol and Arrietta gathered to see what was a wrong with little Bobby, Sally was clearly distressed and said she had tried every remedy she knew, yet still he burned as hot as a blacksmiths fire, Arrietta showed great concern she was found of the strange little human pup and Hartol was clearly worried, he still felt such guilt at tricking his beloved sister Sarah and sending her far away, back in time, Arrietta suggested she took his warm clothes of and submerge him in the cool waters, so Sally carefully did leaving on only his little long johns, little Bobby floated in the water held firmly by Sally and slowly he started to look less flushed and she felt his brow cool, she then lay him on the soft mossy bank, each one looking over him as his little eyes closed and he found sleep, Sally made him dry and covered him in her light cloak, she constantly checked him as they began to talk. Sally thought it was wrong what they were doing and had done, surely and she sobbed for Sarah and Tom, the ghosts of Billy and Lacey had even gone now, the wood was quiet as a blanket of snow, Arrietta agreed and nuzzled little Bobby, she asked Hartol if they could go back for them, he thought it was to dangerous they had to wait for Hugh's command they couldn't ruin what he had done, Arrietta thought though if the book had passed on, then the children had played their part, this Hartol agreed and after several hours of discussion and debate it was agreed, Hartol and Arrietta would pass through the waterfall of time in the morning to see what the Centaurs knew. Sally felt some hope for the return of her friends, she lay by Bobby not daring to move from the waters edge should his fever flare up again, he slept and breathed soundly though, Sally found sleep and when she woke Hartol and Arrietta were gone, Sally prayed out loud and sang her favourite songs, little Bobby woke and giggled at her noise, she rocked him tenderly and wandered, together they found a tasty breakfast. Sally was so relieved he was well and had hope in her heart that Hartol and Arrieitta would do what was right and bring back the children. The woods for the first time in ages felt lonely to Sally, even with dear little Bobby by her side, who began his growling again, she felt an emptiness like the day Meriiti had left her, Sally was more certain than ever that Sarah and Meriiti where the same or connected in some way, she pondered if it was possible and worried that her empty feelings meant that Sarah was in danger. Sally made her way back to her hut and set about making a potion, she needed to see something hopeful, after several hours of mixing, chopping cooking and spells, Sally was ready she carefully placed her potion in her treas-ured silver bowl, Sally lit the swirling oils, Bobby looked on with glee as he saw colours drift up into the sky, then Sally saw the im-ages of Sarah, Tom, Lacey and Billy they sat in a cart pulled by a small pony, then she saw the fear on Sarahs face and she heard hooves and then the picture faded, Sally now felt worse than be-fore she could do nothing to help, she just had to wait and wait, she at least knew though they were in the woods, so close yet so far away. A little later matters were made far worse, she heard a voice echoing in the woods and as it came closer Sally knew the voice, it was poor Tom's Pa, he often wandered the woods calling their names, his calls grew louder as his path came closer and closer, Sally realised he had got to close without Hartol to help change his direction, she had no help, she begged Bobby to be silent, Bobby though heard the call of Sarah and Tom he heard his own name Bobby being called out loud and the bark of Buster, with excite-ment he cried out his signature roar and crawled as quick as light-

ning towards the cries and like a little pup, he sat at the feet of
Tom's Pa, giggling and growling, Tom picked up the infant amazed
to find the little one so bonnie, he did not continue to look for his
captor and instead sharply turned with Bobby in his arms, Buster
sniffed and jumped up at him in joy, he like his master did not care
to search any further that day, tomorrow Tom's Pa would be back
with help, Bobby was proof they were a live, somewhere he believed Tom and Sarah lived, he could feel them and sense they
were near by. Tom's Pa had the strangest dreams that night, he remembered running in the woods and the white stag, he felt he
could reach out and touch the children so close and deep in his
heart he knew, that they were a whisper away yet centuries behind.

BLUFF & BACK 1386

The Centaurs lead the little cart pulled by Struddle through the pretty woodland the mossy paths echoed with the thuds of the heavy hooves, Bauta spoke in his gentle tones to the children and Tom cautiously chatted back, eventually they reached the tranquillity and safety of the Dell, for Tom this was the worse part over, he was glad to get everyone safely into the Dell with no trouble, the monastery would be fully a wake now and their absence would be noted, Hugh was bound to follow soon although Tom prayed he would be thwarted by the return of the Abbot. They still had no time to waste, Sarah began her speech carefully, she had rehearsed it several times in her head, as if she was in a play, she recited her lines and with each word she spun her lie as convincingly as possible, Lacey and Billy were easy to satisfy she was not sure about Bauta though, so grand and sagacious, Sarah with determination looked him straight in the eye and told him, how Hugh had ordered them to go through the waterfall of time, they had to return to the same place several weeks before they had disappeared, had Sarah known the true significance of their return, she would have been far more nervous and if she had known that an army gathered outside Brown Folly Woods, she would never have been able to remain so composed, just as Sarah finished her recital to her complete shock, she saw Hartol and Arrietta walking towards them from the waterfall, Sarah ran to greet them with a hug and in the shortest of times, she spun her lie a little further and with no hesitation Hartol and Arrietta quickly prepared the small group for travel. Tom and Sarah would return on the date Sarah gave, this time though they would be joined by company and with joy and hope, they all walked towards the sparkling waterfall with Hartol as their leader and guide they disappeared from sight leaving the year 1386 and Hugh to his devoted divine intervention, each wondering what they would find in 1721.

EARLY BIRDS 1386

Hugh woke a little later than normal after a night of fretting, he was ready quickly and left this room, Hugh made his way to the stables, he poked his head into Struddles stall, just to pat her and say a little goodbye, when he entered her stall he found it empty, Struddle was missing, confused he had no time to question, instead he tacked up Fleur the grumpy yet speedy chestnut, he would need her pace, soon Hugh was charging towards the river, he took the track that lead north, he wore his habit hood low over his face and would keep himself to himself, with no chatting to any passers by, Hugh needed to vanish, he was unsure if he would be back to the monastery again in its present time, Fleur was good to her reputation and darted along the tracks glad to be free of her stall. Hugh began to wonder as he rode where little Struddle had gone, he hoped maybe she had just been turned out early to grass by Billy or Tom, he knew both doted on the pony, he thought of them with guilt knowing full well he had probably abandoned them for good, he feared he could do nothing for them without others becoming suspicious and asking to many questions of him, he could not just get rid of four children from the monastery without notice. He convinced himself they would be fine and rode on, he hoped he would find the King were he predicted him to be. Hugh was nervous his only protection was the lords cross and his own prayer, he travelled in fear through dangerous shires, with folk that were not gentle or kind and only had theft and violence in their minds, the track was hard going and seemed endless and Hugh questioned his sanity to have embarked alone on such a trip, still he carried on, like many travellers he would follow the rivers

when possible, Hugh lost the meandering Avon and found the less
Serene, yet stupendous Severn as its vast waters joined the estu-
ary, he knew now he had left far behind his home county and com-
forts, his heart felt empty to think of what he would loose, Hugh
fought back tears, he thought he would never falter so much over
what was his life's holy grail, Hugh was so lost in thought and self
pity, that he did not hear the hooves behind him and it was only
when Fleur started to become skittish that he paid more attention, he was soon surrounded by an army of horses with soldiers
in full armour horns blew and drums bellowed, Hugh quickly
pulled Fleur of the track, as she snorted and stamped in distress,
the great army did not even look at the humble monk with the
fiery chestnut and each one stoney faced passed him by, the procession changed to more grand knights and horses so huge they
towered above the flanks of others, then couriers dressed in finery
rode or travelled in carriages, the middle carriage was carved with
fine details and had the crest of the royals on the carriage doors,
they were surrounded by sturdy knights, Hugh got one small
glimpse of the King, the grandeur was humbling and Hugh felt
uneasy being within such close proximity to his highness, yet just
for a second they held each others gaze and Hugh felt his wonder,
he was no longer a mere man with a title, he truly had the air and
wonder of a god. The procession carried on, with other grand carriages with ladies in waiting and the dear yet controversial queen
Anne, who sat sweetly in her carriage adorned with rich fabrics
and furs, men in the holy cloth then rode past, followed by endless
horses pulling carts of weapons and supplies, Hugh could not possibly count but he felt sure the procession was four hundred or
more and to Hugh's great relief his journey was now made simple
and safe as he tucked himself in amongst the horses and carts, no
one would bat an eye at a humble monk they never did and Hugh
now knew for sure he was on track as he smugly sat amongst the
Kings procession, the endless train of horses, carriages and people
seemed it would never stop, Hugh was tired and hungry and was
not sure if Fleur could carry on, finally though they turned of the
river path and drove up a hill, suddenly from nowhere they were

going through huge gates, they clattered across a drawbridge and entered through another gated entrance with a tower on either side, soon they were in an immense courtyard flagged by huge towers that reached to the sky in rose coloured stone and dark wood, the sight was one of both chaos and amazement, Hugh thought quickly what he should do, he marched off with his head down to find some place of worship, something of this size would hold a small chapel at-least, Hugh took Fleur to the stables where a kind boy a little like Billy eagerly took Fleur off to be stabled, watered and fed, Fleur whinnied at the other horses, Hugh seeing that the horses were treated better than most humans, left Fleur content she was to be well cared for, eventually after striding around in amazement, Hugh found a grand chapel, with the same rose tinted walls the door and surround were beautifully carved, the whole castle and grounds had a definite feel of glory and wealth, he nervously entered the chapel, it was cooler yet still bright small arches lead to an altar decorated in flowers and stone candlesticks, the pretty arched windows had simple yet striking pictures of flowers, Hugh ran his hand along the huge tombs on each he read the name Berkley carved into the stone, there was a huge crest above the altar arch, with white horses rearing and the same flowers that were on the windows, with the name Berkley decoratively painted, Hugh could only presume he was in the chapel of Berkley castle, he sat on a pew and knelt to pray, for what he was not sure, forgiveness, success or solace, as Hugh raised his head a young curate appeared from the entrance of the bell tower, the curate looked quizzically at him, he then strode over with confidence and a smile, Hugh stood to greet him, admiring his chapel and telling the curate where he was from, with no mention of what he was doing. The curate named Peter happily chatted excitedly as he had been to the monastery at Bath as a child, so they happily chatted about the monks they both knew and the wonders of the hot spring water and plentiful food. Without question Peter told Hugh much of the Berkley family and Berkley castle and how they had always been in favour with the royals for generations and often held court, he did mumble, he was surprised King Richard had visited with his rumblings of distaste towards most of the aristocracy. Hugh avoided the conversation and asked Peter if he knew where he may sleep for the night, Peter happily offered him a spare cot in the priest house and explained sadly priest Bartholomew had passed away only a few weeks ago and they thought to replace him with Peter, only as he was so accommodating and less strict on the families slight adjustments to the religious ways, Hugh laughed at his wording and decided he liked Peter and felt certain he was safe in his company, he however did have to come up with a reason for being let out of the monastery and on what business. Peter told Hugh the castle routines and invited him to dine with him in the priest house, away from the great halls and kitchens, this to Hugh was a huge relief, so Hugh accepted graciously and then excused himself saying he had some business to attend to and walked of with purpose. Hugh walked around the kitchen gardens admiring the produce, if not a little limiting he thought, he then wandered towards the castle and with no questions walked through the great halls, each with huge fire places and intricate carvings, tapestries hung on the walls and huge pieces of wooden furniture did little to fill the rooms, Hugh heard footsteps and quickly put his head down as if in prayer, a sharp voice behind him ask for his business and to Hugh's complete shock he turned to see the King, Hugh without thought answered he was there to bless the rooms and rid them of any evil spirits, the King eyed him suspiciously, then bid him to sit and talk, it seemed the monk was a perfect find for the King, he had so many questions to ask of a truly religious man, fate could not have worked in a better way for Hugh or the King that day, for from the moment they spook to each other, their conversation flowed like a song, they understood each other in completeness and an accidental meeting became an unbreakable bond. All the time Hugh spoke to the King he felt like he spoke to Hector the godly monk and never would he shake that feeling, he would always see hector in the King. Hugh excused himself for his supper in the priests house, so impressed by Hugh, the King asked him to travel with him in his carriage to Shrewsbury they had much to discuss, the King then retired with his thoughts to the comfort of his chambers, Hugh walked back to the priest house dumfounded by what had just happened, he now was the kings religious council and every word the king had spoken meant that he followed the book of Moirai and he intended to follow its beliefs and understanding of the world. As Hugh sat in the grand carriage the following morning, he reflected on his wonderful supper with Peter and how he had truly made a friend and now refreshed with no nerves he spoke freely to King, giving him wholesome honest answers, each fitting the need the King had, the King a clever man soon began to realise that Hugh knew much of this prophecy and he also understood his problems of implementing a new way, the people were hungry for progression and this Hugh had thought of often and had many surprising solutions for the King on how peoples lives could be enriched and improved, after all Hugh had seen the future he knew they already had enough they just needed to make things more civilised, fairer and more comfortable. The King was so impressed with his knew acquaintance that he immediately made Hugh his first council and by the time, the carriage rattled onto the cobbles of the sleepy mid England town on the Severn, an alliance so strong and knowledgeable had been made, between one godly king and one not so simple monk. Hugh looked at the little cottages in neat streets and saw the children running in excitement, a young girl like Lacey drew him back to his humble start and he thought he now had the power to return to them soon and get Sarah and Tom home to Bobby and as he thought this thought, a vivid image flashed into his head, he saw a small army of angry villagers at the woods edge and despite his internal panic there was nothing he could do.

BACK TO BROWN FOLLY WOODS

Sally paced the woods in fear, she saw through Eudes the mob gather outside the line of trees, she knew each had weapons and meant harm, they now looked for Sarah, Tom and their captors and she would be hung for certain if caught, Sally ran towards the Dell no one was around Artu and his heard had been gone for a few days to some other time and Hartol and Arrietta had still not returned, she feared they would not be back in time for Sally, Sally thought to cross the fountain but she remembered Meriiti's words, she could never cross, Sally did not understand why she could not use the fountain of time like so many others, Meriiti had mentioned something of a black moon and how the Gods would not let her through and keep her instead for eternity in the dark world between, so Sally paced and prayed the Dell would protect her, she curled up in the huge oak tree's branches and waited for her fate. As Sally slept in the oak tree, a huge storm gathered outside and the army of men ready to strike and search were struck by hail and lightning, they fiercely pushed on into the wood, with every step they took the wind picked up and the hail grew larger, forks of lighting shattered down between the trees as if it were loaded from a gun, defeated and in fear the men dropped their weapons and ran, again the woods had won and as the men went back to the village with its smoky chimneys and candle lit rooms, each bedraggled and deflated looked up to see a strange light never seen before in the sky, the deepest violet with silver flashes shone above them, everyone came out and to see at first, then the flashes grew stronger and in haste they ran back to their homes and shelter, each terrified of what was to become of them. Sally heard the war of the storm outside her nest and she muttered and prayed and then she glimpsed through dazzling lights Hartol and Arrietta, tears rolled down her face in relief and behind them dear Sarah and Tom followed hand in hand and then a sweet little pony and cart and sat at the helm proud and grinning Billy and Lacey, yet not the Billy and Lacey, Sally once knew, their ghostly figures were now replaced with glowing flesh and hair, sparkling eyes and voices not whispers, strong and real, she ran from her perch to great them and warned them of the pack of villagers, Hartol shook his grand head though and stated all trouble was gone and would not be back, the year was 1721 and different now, Sally didn't understand, none of them did really not yet, it would take the discovery of the new life for them to see. Hartol asked them to go home and return in a few days, he turned and went back towards the fountain with Arrietta close behind they disappeared. Sally asked Lacey and Billy to come with her, so they all hopped into the cart and had a bumpy track ride to Sally's hovel, something was different about the wood it felt thicker and more ancient trees stood taller and stouter, they heard different animal cries and to their joy they saw the Centaurs in the distance running freely with no care, as they turned the corner to glade where Sally's humble abode lay, they stopped in disbelief, instead a small farm stood with a pretty cottage, stable and barn with a lovely sweeping paddock and neat gardens that drifted to the stream, Sally quickly ran to see who had taken her land and hut only to find that it was her's, with her own belongings and many more, strange lights hung from the walls, and wonderful fabric chairs of different shapes scattered the rooms, a table was set and a warm range stood in the chimney breast upon it a small cauldron cooked something that smelt wonderful, she went upstairs and a huge bed stood with endless fabric throws and pillows, the house felt warm and clean and then Sally saw her reflection in the glass her hair was neatly pinned and she wore a fine long dress with a warm knit her skin felt soft and her nails were clean, she ran outside to see her neat garden, vegetables and chickens, she now had a dairy cow, a water well and a barn full of neatly stacked sweet yellow hay and sacks upon sacks of grain, the children ran behind touching everything to check it was real, Sarah heard the chimes of the church bells peeling out like they had never heard before. All of them got into the cart and headed to the village, the track was smoother and little Struddle flew along, they entered the village and were shocked to see more of the same, the tiny cottages all replaced by little small holdings, it seemed everyone had beautiful big cottages with gardens, paddocks, barns and stables, each with the same light brown pretty dairy cows, Sarah saw her own cottage was so much bigger they had lambs running in the paddock and a huge garden could be seen, she wanted to look but knew they had to get to the church, something told them they all had to be there, the church was much the same only when they walked in it was lighter and warmer, beautiful music played from wonderful instruments, they were greeted with joy by the vicar and they went to sit and realised their families sat in neat rows, Tom and Sarah looked at each other and tears fell down their rosy cheeks, for sat there as large as life was little Mary with her Ma and Pa and Bobby who coed and giggled in her Ma's arms and Tom looked to see his beloved Ma with the baby Mary sleeping softly in her arms and his Pa doting over them both, each family turned with smiles to greet them, laughing, why did they always have to be so late, Sarah heard Mother Darcey's booming voice say, those two will be late for their own weddings and funerals no doubt, people laughed, Tom and Sarah quickly took their seats, they then sat through the most amazing sermon, Sarah sat with a certain sense of relief, they still had God and much was the same it seemed, although there was a good spirit amongst the village she did not remember and a look of contentment on peoples faces, she could not help but stare at Tom's older brother Guy his face once wore stains from the stone mines and a permanent grimace, he now looked soft and sat closely to a girl with an infant who he gloated at through out the sermon. The church service floated around Sarah as though she was in a dream and she left with her family waving to Sally, Lacey and Billy who hesitated by the rackety cart pulled by Struddle. Her Ma and Pa chatted to others and then asked Sarah if she would introduce them to the new arrivals, Sarah quickly and proudly with her fingers crossed behind her back, did just so and her Ma chatted to Sally Woods and her two wards Billy and Lacey Woods, Sarah went to Tom and squeezed his hand amongst the crowd to check all was real he grinned with a low ouch and told her it was real, he beamed to see his Ma and baby Mary breathing the air and his Pa's happy face, they said farewell to Lacey and Billy and all agreed to meet soon at Sally's in the woods, all were intrigued to explore there new homes and lives. Sarah beamed happiness to see Lacey and Billy look so thrilled and Sally finally had her own little family to love, she pinched herself a dozen times when she looked at little Mary, who giggled and danced her way home. Sarah found it hard to say goodbye to Tom who gently cradled his baby sister Mary, he looked so confident and self assured there was something almost saintly about him and Sarah gasped to herself he was just like one of the knights in the book, she had stolen glimpses of, that night in the monastery and then he looked at her as if they both now knew, this was always going to be their path Sarah and Tom both from another time, chosen once by the Gods lived on. They tore their glances away from each other, both knowing they would never be apart for long.

BROTHER HUGH A LATE RETURN

King Richard of England met with his opposition, his parliament and counsellors, with a monk at his side, many attended mostly powerful men with a mixture of greed, stature, devotion and deceit stood in the cathedral, all under the eye of God, while the King set out his new and complex plans for parliament and the country, his rules were at times confusing to some and the good parliament stood aghast, yet everything he said gave them everything they wanted for the poor and the rich, after several hours of debate and acceptance, the King announced he now must talk with the King of France Charles, the war between England and France was to be over, he had drawn up a peaceful treaty, that he knew was agreeable, money and man power could be saved for better things than death and poverty. Whispers and sighs could be heard through out the walls of the cathedral, as the aghast struggled with such news, they had hope and confusion, word would spread across the land quickly the King was behaving like he was a god. Hugh soon after sought permission for a short leave to sort a problem he had not attended to, the King agreed with ease and the new partners wished each other well and agreed to meet again soon. Hugh left the cobbled streets a different man, no longer a true monk he would soon leave his habit behind, he could not quite believe all that had happened and how well like clock work everything worked, he thought of the King and how he was devoted to him and excited to spend his time with the god like figure, who he felt sure was Hector, as he pondered so many thoughts Hugh realised he had been in the saddle for hours, he had not rested once, he eventually made it back to the castle where he had left Fleur, he felt some sense of relief, he rode knowing it was his last chance of freedom before his return to work with the King. The King rode to France with an army of peace makers, he sent out into the world many messengers each with the same wax sealed document, from the King, he was to create a new way for mankind and a prophecy that would be followed, an impossible task, yet strangely the time was perfect as the world struggled with hunger and wars, many believed it was a sign from the Gods, word spread quickly of the god like king, who sought peace and freedom for all. Hugh wondered how the King would manage his task and felt such pride to be the chosen one for his deepest council. At Berkley Castle Hugh sought out his friend Peter, he asked him to help with his new work for the King, Hugh knew he could trust him, he felt like an old friend, Peter was unsure at first, then excitedly he accepted exchanging a life of humdrum and religious service to a wealthy family, for one of excitement and change, to Hugh he was a perfect scholar of his religion, who could help to maintain the bible in the new world to come. Peter agreed to meet Hugh at the new moon on a summers eve, with found farewells Hugh left eager to get back to the monastery. Fleur's hooves felt the soft turf and sweet smell of the valleys she was off, with an eager burst of energy after a long rest, his ride home was pleasant and fast, Hugh entered the calm lanes of the city leading to the monastery, Fleur trotted eagerly towards home, Hugh greeted many familiar faces and the thought struck him, these humble folk would never know any different they would live their lives in more comfort, with less disease and hunger, they would take this enormous change to the future with no understanding ever of what had happened, Hugh was excited to be able to set Tom and Sarah free. As he walked back into the monastery whispers and gazes followed his path, he was called almost immediately by the Abbot, the Abbot sat in his dark office hunched over his books, his slits for eyes slyly peered at Hugh as he entered, he reminded Hugh of a rotund rat, who sat with to many spoils, to lazy to move on or care, the Abbot wasted no time his questions came fast with a fierce under tone. Hugh replied as much as he wished although gave little away, he excused himself and much to the Abbot's disbelief left without waiting to be dismissed, Hugh knew this and his attitude would rial him beyond his capability of calm and would bring on some display of anger or violence, like an explosion the Abbot responded in away that even surprised Hugh, Hugh walked out purposely into the dusky light of the cloisters and to the crowd of monks who gathered before their evening song, the Abbot came running after Hugh demanding him to return and in his hand he wheeled a large axe, normally used to split the logs, gasps and shouts to Hugh could be heard, as the Abbot tried to bring the axe down on Hugh. Hugh quickly dodged and the axe bared down on the poor statue of the dear St Benedict. Cry's surrounded the cloisters, Hugh began to think the monks would have preferred it to have been his head, instead of the precious statue, disregarding his own self pity and shock, he quickly helped seize the Abbot, who was swiftly locked in the small turret room, used as punishment for disobedient monks, the monks then all hurried to the chapter house to discuss what was to be done. All in shock from drama, they talked long in to the evening and listened to Hugh taking his council, it was agreed the Abbot could no longer be trusted in the walls of the monastery, it was arranged for him to go and live in a half way house, out in the woods a small country priory at Hinton, where he could be watched and left to do minimal tasks. A new Abbot would be arranged by the archbishop and Hugh explained his knew role as a council to the King, he then said he had found the family of Sarah and Tom so would take them with him, the monks looked at him with confusion and said they had left nearly a week a ago, under his orders according to the stable hand, who had helped them tack Struddle to the cart. Hugh could not believe yet another twist had transpired, it appeared both Lacey and Billy were gone too, he would have left immediately only the skies were dark with no moon and he felt so weary, he explained to the monks he would be gone early in the morning and bid them all well with their new Abbot, he hoped to see them again soon. Hugh slept like a log and woke early he packed and headed back to the stables, he found himself a fresh horse, in disbelief again Hugh was in the saddle, this time upon the sturdy black mare named Midnight, who happily trotted out of the city and towards the woods, she stole many mouthfuls of hedge or sweet grass she could and sniffed at the early morning air, Hugh knew the woods well and headed towards the Centaurs in hope they would track him quickly so he could get answers, he was still not sure if this was where the children had fled, whatever had happened though it seemed he could not stop Billy and Lacey running to the woods. Irritatingly the Centaurs took their time to come the one time Hugh needed them, eventually though they sought out Hugh and Midnight, to Hugh's dismay only a few young ones were sent, he needed to talk to Bauta, he needed to know where the children were. When Hugh arrived at the Dell he still had no answers, Bauta was gone. Exhausted by the past days of travel and so much change, he patiently lay on the mossy branches of the huge oak tree and waited.

SARAH THE PRINCESS
OF THE WOODS

Sarah woke early the next morning, the sun streamed through her window and the early morning breeze blew her new pretty curtains, her room was wonderful with soft sheets and fluffy pillows, she had a huge rug that nearly covered the floor and a thick curtain by the door, blankets were neatly folded at the bottom of her bed and she had cupboard full of warm and cooler clothes and a pretty blue thick wool coat with matching hat and mittens, she had a mirror and sewing box and flower press, with books next to them on a neat shelf and lights by her bed, the house had a bathing room she could have hot water when ever she wanted, the whole house continued in a comfortable and luxurious way, they had food on the table and in the cupboards and everything felt dry and not damp, she looked out at the pretty flower and herb garden and then the wonderful vegetables and fruits, the orchard and paddocks with chickens, sheep, a cow and some pigs, Sarah went downstairs to see Bobby who eagerly went to her smiling and gurgling not growling, little Mary played on the soft rug looking at a pretty book, she had rosy cheeks and was lovely and plump instead of skinny and pale, Sarah's Ma happily busied herself and they all sat to a huge bowl of porridge with apple and honey, Sarah's Ma asked her if she would go over to Tom's she had sorted some baby clothes for baby Mary and made them a cherry pie, she said Bobby and Mary were having there special medicine at the Doctors, to stop them getting Scarlett fever and some other nasty diseases, Sarah asked if she would get the medicine and her Ma looked at her dumbstruck, Sarah had had two lots already when she was Bobby and Mary's age, her Ma teased her and Sarah laughed it off, she did however realise both her and Tom had problem, they had lived a life they knew nothing about and were some how going to have to blag their way through, Sarah watched as her cheerful Ma put Bobby in the most amazing looking cart called a pram, she saw Mary do the buckles on her beautiful soft shoes worn over lovely little socks, her Ma laughed again, asking her to hurry with the clothes and cherry pie, so obediently Sarah quickly put on her own wonderful shoes nearly banging into several things as he stared at them so. She then ran as fast as she could to Tom's cottage that was thankfully in the same place just much bigger, Tom eagerly greeted her and they whispered they would meet in the woods, Sarah took the clothes and pie inside to find Tom's Ma, she sat in the most wonderful kitchen swinging on rocking chair, singing to her little baby, Sarah went to look at the baby Mary she had rose bud lips pink cheeks and plump little hands and wrists like her Mary, Sarah couldn't help but ask if she had had the medicine and Tom's Ma replied she would get more when she was Bobby's age, in disbelief Sarah sat and just stared at the delicate bundle, while Tom's Ma happily looked through the pretty clothes, they then all had a piece of the cherry pie with thick cream, once a delicacy that would have only been eaten on a very special occasion. Sarah and Tom escaped running to the woods and towards the Dell bursting with joy, they called for Lacey and Billy, every so often they would stop and dance laughing, then both would stop and look at each other intensely knowing they had done it, they had made the baby Mary, little Mary and Tom's ma live. As they ran they saw the Fauns running in a huge herd through Brown Folly Woods, Arrietta and Artu were proudly prancing at the front and then to their amazement they saw the Centaurs with Bauta and Hartol, stamping at the ground, they looked around them and realised Brown Folly Woods was no longer the same, it was an ancient woodland with forgotten fauna and foliage it teamed with wildlife and the whole place felt like the Dell, they made their way from memory along the familiar little moss paths, to their joy the black bird scuttled and flew in front of them, just as he had on their first visit, they arrived into the deep thicket that surrounded the Dell and walked in with as much wonderment as they had the very first time, only this time things were not still and quiet the place bustled with activity, both people and creatures travelled back and forth through the fountains of time bringing knowledge, seeds and inventions of a different time, it had become the fountain of knowledge and Sarah and Tom began to understand how they had become so advanced in some ways, while other ways had never been permitted to happen, Sarah went over to the crystal pool and drank, she patted her face with the magical water, when she rose she was greeted by Hartol and to her pleasure and surprise Hugh stood meekly behind him with his head down, expecting a curt response from Sarah and Tom, all had worked out well though and they were over joyed to see him, they sat together as Hugh told them tales of his journey and about the book of Moirai, the King and the Abbot, he admired Sarah and Tom for their bravery and resolve, although he was still unsure about Lacey and Billy, when he saw them though running towards him in the Dell with Sally and Struddle close behind, he grinned from ear to ear and thanked Sarah and Tom, Sally was so thrilled to be back with everyone, she missed Bobby, Sarah explained though he was just a normal baby boy, who was quite boring he didn't growl or do anything strange. The companions stayed together, Arrietta joined them with Artu and Bauta even showed his face for a short while before the gallops called him back, Sally made Sarah a flower garland and placed it on her, she said she was the princess of the woods, Sarah accepted her role laughing, deep down though she felt she knew and understood things that she could not explain, she some how felt connected and knew she had a job to do. Sarah and Tom would travel through the fountain again many times in their lives, with Brother Hugh's guidance they followed his prophecy from the book of Moirai, history and events had all changed, the world would now always be a different place and maybe some things were never found and some amazing things never happened but the world was safe, quiet, calm and full of natural wonders.

THE END

Written and Illustrated By Victoria J Hunt ©

22/12/2021

This story is fictional it contains some historical, beliefs, information and places that are used in a fictional manner only and may
not be always be factual or accurate.